The Cowboy's Heart

The Cowboy's Heart

A Three Sisters Ranch Romance

Jamie K. Schmidt

TULE
PUBLISHING

Chapter One

J ANICE SULLIVAN PAUSED long enough under the mistletoe that Nate Pierson should have gotten the hint. He was as dense as a doorknob, sometimes. Nate had jammed himself into a corner with his arms folded, obviously annoyed. Janice knew this because he was awake. He also hated crowds and had to be dragged here, practically kicking and screaming, by his ranch hands. He squinted over at her from beneath his wide Stetson and scowled. He was a man of few words, but endless glares and snarls.

Merry Christmas to you, too.

Holding in an exasperated sigh, she moved toward Emma Corbyn who was handing out eggnog by a huge punch bowl.

"Please tell me this is spiked," Janice said, gratefully accepting it.

"It wouldn't be a tree trimming without it. Although, you missed the huge fight we had over what to spike it with."

Janice took a sip and hummed in approval. "Rum."

Emma raised her glass. "You're welcome. Amelia wanted to use this snooty brandy and Delilah wanted whiskey. While they were arguing, I dumped in a bottle of Appleton's."

"Not all heroes wear capes," Janice said and moved along so other people could get some. As she waited in line to talk with Lily Corbyn, Janice tried to find some Christmas cheer. The tree was enormous and sparkled with colored and white lights. Silver and gold tinsel accented the modern glass as well as the antique wooden ornaments. The annual Corbyns' Christmas-tree-trimming party was in full swing. Half the town was already here and the other half was on their way. A little furl of excitement tickled her stomach and for a few moments, she was a kid again counting down the days to Santa's visit.

Twenty-five.

And then it was a fast sleigh ride into the new year. A new year filled with happy events, like her two sisters' weddings and new opportunities, like a wind farm and a wildlife safari on their land. Unfortunately, none of that was Janice's doing. She was still struggling to get her women's retreat center up and running. And the only man she had ever been interested in marrying was too caught up in working for her father to give her a chance.

As if Nate sensed her thoughts, he looked up from the stuffed date he had popped in his mouth and gave her a wink. Hot and cold. Feast or famine. She and Nate had been dancing around a mutual attraction that had started out as forbidden fruit and turned into a long-distance thing and then the fire was banked. Except when it wasn't.

He confused and infuriated her, and Janice wasn't sure what to do. Realizing that Lily was watching her watch Nate,

Janice slurped her eggnog to cover her embarrassment. "The tree is gorgeous," Janice said, wondering if she had a cream mustache.

"Thank you, dear. Are you here with Nate?"

"We all came together." Janice nonchalantly dabbed at her upper lip. Her sister Kelly and Kelly's fiancé Trent were chatting with Doctor McBride and his wife Bella over by the cookies. Trent and Kelly's five-year-old daughter, Alissa, was munching on a gingerbread boy and looking to snitch a peanut butter blossom while the adults were talking. Janice pretended she didn't see it and turned back to Lily.

"Thank you for inviting us. Coming here is like the official start of the Christmas season."

Lily smiled. "I'm glad you feel that way. We think so too."

Janice didn't want to monopolize her hostess's time, so she headed over to the next room where soft holiday music was playing. A few couples were swaying together. Her baby sister Emily and Emily's fiancé Donovan were grinning up at each other, lost in each other's eyes. Looking somewhere else, Janice tried to force down the pang of jealousy that took away from her budding holiday spirit. She wished her sisters all the happiness in the world. But when was it going to be her turn?

Searching around for Nate, she found him stocking up on shrimp cocktail and pigs in a blanket. As she was about to stalk over to him and demand that he dance with her to Greg Lake's "I Believe in Father Christmas," her father stepped in and took her arm.

"Hey," he said. "I've got good news."

Janice forced down her annoyance at his timing and drained her eggnog in one gulp. "Glad to hear it."

"I was just talking with Boomer Tucker's cousin Phil and he said his wife's friend's brother is looking for riding lessons."

Janice's head swirled from too much rum too fast and trying to untangle the connections in that last sentence. "Okay," she said.

"I thought you'd feel that way. He's coming in tomorrow morning around eight. I told him you'd be happy to give him riding lessons."

"I would?" Janice said.

"It's not like you're doing anything else." Frank Sullivan patted her on the arm and went back into the crowd.

The depressing part was, he was right. She was going to have to face facts that the retreat center she'd dumped all her money into was a disaster. If she didn't start diversifying with something else, she was going to default on her loan. And that terrified her because she had put her prized horses up as collateral. She had done it to help save the Three Sisters Ranch from bankruptcy. Her sisters had pitched in with their own projects, but so far, they had been more successful than Janice.

She had been in Kentucky enjoying assisting the veterinarian at a dressage farm, when she got the voice mail from her father.

Come home one last time. We're selling the ranch. We can't keep up with the bills.

Panicked, Janice had called her sisters and over several phone calls, they came up with ways they could pull the ranch out of the red. Emily was going to use a few empty pastures and build wind turbines on them. Kelly rented out space on the ranch for a portrait studio, while Janice took out a loan to lease land from her father to build her retreat center on. Her parents had rented out even more land to Trent Campbell and Donovan Link. All together, they were slowly making headway on the bills, but they weren't out of the woods yet.

She couldn't bear to think of them losing the ranch. It meant so much to her, so much to all of her family. If they were foreclosed on, Janice didn't know anywhere else she could call home. Every little thing from gathering eggs to making sure the animals were fed and watered every day made her feel a part of something larger—like she had a place in this world. Her retreat center would help other women who needed that type of validation in their lives.

If she could get anyone to sign up for it.

"Janice, you look beautiful."

Whirling around, she saw their veterinarian Pete Dickerson had come up behind her and offered her a glass of punch.

"Oh, I didn't know you had one," he said with a slight flush of embarrassment.

"I could always use another one." She took the punch from him and sipped it, this time. No sense in getting tipsy this early in the evening. "You're looking very spiffy yourself."

"Thank you, ma'am," he drawled.

Pete had kind, brown eyes and laugh lines that creased the edges of them. He was a tall thin man, with rangy muscles and a wide grin. His sandy-blond hair was cut and styled professionally, unlike a lot of the ranch hands and farmers around them. His Italian suit stood out as well. Pete was a damned good vet, but he didn't seem to belong here in Texas. He reminded her of the big city.

"How's business?" she asked.

"You know how it is. I'm all over the place."

Pete went from farm to farm in his van. He had said he liked not being tied down to an office. If she hadn't hated being a large-animal vet, she would have asked him if he needed a helper. She could work a few hours and try to stay ahead of the bills. She didn't really want to be working with the cattle or farm animals, though. Horses, she could deal with. They were usually loved and protected by their owners—around here anyway. Cattle, on the other hand, were viewed as a commodity. Sometimes people forgot that they were animals too, and not just marks on a ledger.

Janice hated the way cattlemen treated their stock. She knew that made her sound a little like Emily, but it was true. There was no need to be brutal to the cows, even if they were just going to the slaughterhouse in the spring.

They stared at each other in awkward silence. Pete rocked back and forth. Maybe she should ask him to dance? She liked him. He was kind. He loved animals. Maybe it was time to move on from her girlish crush? She bit her lip. She wished she wasn't so awkward at this. How hard would it be to look him in the eye and ask him to dance?

Why didn't he ask her?

"How is your retreat going?" he asked.

Not the question she was looking for. Janice tried to stop the grimace, but he caught it.

"That bad, huh?"

"I think I'm going to have to come up with something else."

"I'm sorry," he said, cupping her elbow. "I know how much this means to you."

She took a bracing sip of her punch. "It does. It really does. I didn't want to give up."

"Then don't. Something will come up. Something always does."

Janice wondered if Miles Honeyman was looking to add to his staff. She didn't want the tree-trimming party to turn into a networking event, but he was the only local veterinarian who concentrated on dogs and cats, and smaller animals. Janice wouldn't mind working with them. But there wasn't a lot of money in it and that wouldn't help save her family's ranch.

She needed to find some income that would keep the ranch ahead of the bills until Emily's wind farm started giving them a return on their investment.

Pete was about to say more, but three ranchers came up and started talking about the problems they were having with their herds. This was a party and the last thing she wanted to do was talk shop. As soon as she could, Janice broke away from the group. She blew out a sigh of relief and headed toward the tree.

She couldn't wait to put their tree up, but they always did it Christmas Eve. Maybe she could convince her family to put it up after the parade. They could all use a little more Christmas this year.

"What was all that about?" Nate asked, approaching her and standing way too close because personal space didn't mean a damned thing to him.

Normally she liked that, liked the almost touch of his strong body and the aura of heat and protection he seemed to engulf her with. This close, when she was in a thin cocktail dress and he was dressed in rodeo formal, it felt different, shivery and delicious. It was hard to breathe when he was so close, but she couldn't step away from him.

Janice forced down all the ridiculous butterflies in her stomach and was determined to stare into his gorgeous brown eyes and not make a fool out of herself.

"What?" she asked, cursing the wispy way she said it.

"Pete and your father. What did they want?"

"Pete just wanted to say hi, but my dad got me a client."

"Frank found you a woman in need of a retreat?"

"A man in need of horseback-riding lessons, but close enough." She took a deep breath and screwed up the courage to ask him to dance. Maybe if they did a few turns around the dance floor, tongues would start wagging and Nate would get a clue that they should be more than just friends. That she had fallen in love with him when they were kids and what had started as puppy love had grown into the real thing. At least, for her.

"You got punch all over your lip," Nate wiped his napkin roughly over her face.

Because that was romantic as all get-out.

"Shit," he said.

"Shit?" she repeated.

"I uh smeared your lipstick and now you look like the Joker."

Janice smacked him in the chest with her empty punch glass and stormed off to the bathroom to repair the damages.

Chapter Two

THE NEXT DAY Janice clenched her fist and watched the big Cadillac fishtail as it drove out of the ranch. There went next month's loan payment and the only interest she'd had in her retreat center. All because the jerkface couldn't keep his hands to himself and Nate couldn't keep his temper under control.

Blinking back scalding hot tears, she hated that when she got mad, she didn't scream at the top of her lungs like her sister Kelly, or puff up like an angry cat and get in someone's face like her baby sister Emily did. Nope. When Janice was furious, angry tears spilled down her cheeks.

"Aw, Janice," Nate said, swiping off his hat. "I wasn't yelling at you. Please, don't cry."

"This is an emotional reaction. It is not a weakness," she blubbered. "This is my body's defense, stopping me from kicking the tar out of stubborn assholes like you." Janice finished by whipping off her cat's-eye glasses and wiping her sleeve across her face, which only succeeded in getting dirt in her eyes. "I don't need your help. I didn't ask for it. I don't want it."

"Fine," he said, glaring at her.

She slumped against the barn, feeling like a balloon whose knot came undone. Damn it. When she gave up her career as a vet tech to a dressage farm to help her parents' ranch become more solvent, Janice knew that her plans were going to ruffle Nate's feathers. He was the foreman of the ranch, in charge of the cattle and the ranch hands. She had built a retreat for women who wanted to get back to nature and learn about becoming self-reliant in a country setting. However, the last thing Nate needed or wanted was a bunch of "city slickers" traipsing all over his area. Janice had hoped that he would just ignore the guests when they came. Except no one ever answered her ads or even inquired about using the retreat center.

She figured after all the eggnog he'd had last night, Nate wouldn't have remembered that she was starting horseback-riding lessons this morning. But she should have known better. Nate never forgot—or ignored—anything.

Especially if it involved her.

But only to a certain degree. Just when she thought he would loosen up and maybe ask her to dinner, he pulled back. She should be used to it by now. It'd been like that since they were both sixteen years old. One minute he'd give her a kiss good night that would curl her toes, and the next minute, he'd be the same old grumpy Nate.

Still, she didn't want him to scare off potential clients—even if they got a little handsy. It wasn't the first time a man had slapped her ass. She would have preferred to have handled it herself. But before she could turn around and confront the creep, Nate had hauled him back by his collar.

He'd told the guy to get the hell out of his sight before he "kicked his ass so hard, he'd have to take off his fake New York City Stetson to shit."

And then the man left, taking fifteen hundred dollars' worth of riding lessons and a potential quarterly contract with him. So much for her Christmas miracle.

"We don't need his money anyway."

"Yes, Nate. Yes, we do." Janice put her glasses back on and glowered at Nate. The Three Sisters Ranch needed more income to pay the bills and she needed to make sure she made her loan payments on time.

"You want me to go tell your daddy what that wannabe cowboy just did?"

Dear Lord, no. Her father was one argument away from another heart attack. Frank Sullivan was unapologetically a pain in the ass and had a stubborn streak that sometimes showed itself as mean and callous. But she loved her daddy. All her sisters did. Still, none of them had wanted to be on the bad side of his temper. It had gotten worse as he had gotten older and realized that he couldn't spend twelve hours a day in the saddle anymore. Or that his bones were weaker and broke more easily. Then, it had been his ticker. You would have thought that the first heart attack would have slowed him down.

It had. For a while.

Then while she'd been at a competition, she'd gotten her father's message about selling the ranch.

Sell the Three Sisters Ranch? Over her and her two sisters' dead bodies. Together, they had come up with separate plans on ways to make the ranch more viable. Kelly and Janice had planned to rent land from their father and build their own businesses. Kelly was going to open up a portrait studio and Janice had an idea for a women's retreat center.

"Like a dudette ranch?" Emily had said.

"No!"

But the name had stuck.

Janice wanted a retreat where women who had lost their confidence could get it back by doing things they had never done before—ride a horse, camp out, cook over an open fire…live the life of a cowgirl for a week.

The bank loved the idea—as long as she put up her horses for collateral and still brought in a paycheck from the dressage ranch in Kentucky.

Coughing, Janice hoped the little fib she'd told about that wouldn't be noticed. After the paperwork had been signed and the loan funded, she quit her job in Kentucky and drove cross-country back home to Last Stand, Texas, with her horses and her six dogs. Nate had even helped her move. She really should cut him some slack. It wasn't his fault he was overprotective of her. Her father had practically drilled it into him and all the other ranch hands.

"I can handle a jerk like that," Janice said, trying for a reasonable tone, even though her breath kept hitching as she attempted to will away the tears.

"You shouldn't have to."

"Preach," she said. "But it's not the first time and it won't be the last time."

"Wanna bet?" Nate stepped in closer, looming over her

so she had to tilt her head back to look up into his dark brown eyes that simmered like pissed-off coffee. He smelled like wood smoke and pine. Janice could feel the heat coming off him and she put her hand on his chest to hold him off. The soft chamois under her fingers tempted her to soothe his temper by smoothing her hand over his taut muscles. Hooking his arm around her waist, he brought her into a quick hug. Just like that, her tears dried up and her nerves settled, because it felt so damn right to be in his arms.

"I'm just looking out for you, darlin'."

Janice gave a shaky sigh. She liked when he forgot she wasn't off-limits. She and Nate had been doing this dance since they'd been in high school, and he'd come to work for her father. Frank Sullivan had put the fear of God into Nate, way back when, that his daughters were off-limits. Almost eleven years later, Nate still had "too much respect" for her father to ask her out.

"Look, it's not that I don't appreciate the sentiment," Janice said. "I would have liked to crack the guy across the face myself."

Stepping back, Nate held up his fist and pointed to his first two knuckles. "Hit with these two, don't tuck in your thumb, just like we taught you."

That's what he took away from the situation? Janice sighed. "Just back off. I can take care of myself. If I need help, I'll ask for it? Okay?"

Nate grunted. "Suit yourself." He turned and walked out of the barn.

"Shit." She had offended him.

This wasn't her day. Her only client had been rightfully run off. Nate's nose was out of joint because she hadn't swooned in thanks, like a ninny. It was bad enough she'd cried. And she wasn't any closer to helping her parents save their five-thousand-acre cattle ranch.

Her older sister Kelly and her fiancé Trent had given them all some breathing room when Trent bought some land from her father to build their house on and run his bull-riding school. Kelly had been going to put her portrait studio in Janice's retreat building. But instead, she decided it was easier to set up shop at Trent's school so she could take candid photos of the students on their horses.

Which left Janice on her own to set up her retreat center. Sure, her sisters helped, but they were busy with their own projects. Her younger sister Emily might be the one to save the ranch singlehandedly with her wind turbine farm, but it would take a while to build them and bring in the rent from the wind power they were harnessing. In the meantime, it was up to Janice and Kelly to keep the ranch in the black while Nate and his cowhands did their job.

Staring at the stiff lines of Nate's back as he stormed away, she wished things were easier between them. After they graduated high school, Janice had approached her father about his feelings if she dated his foreman. Her father told her that he liked Nate just fine, but they would never be happy together.

"You're too different," Frank had said. "You're sensitive and he's not. He's committed to this ranch and you have other plans."

It had been a slight dig that she didn't want to continue her education to become a large-animal veterinarian. And then he pushed it even further, because her father didn't do subtle. "If Nate cried every time a steer died, nothing would ever get done."

To be fair, she'd cried *once*. She had been a kid and had nursed the steer through its bout with red nose, an infectious respiratory disease. Janice had been so proud of herself, but the steer hadn't made it. It should have rested some more, but her father wanted it back out there and took the word of their veterinarian over his sixteen-year-old daughter. She had been so angry. Her father and the vet had treated that steer like it wasn't a sentient creature. She'd burst into tears, but not in sadness. It had been a pure and righteous rage.

Of course, her father thought she was crying because she was sad. Janice had been sad, but it was the frustration of being powerless to stop something she knew was wrong. Her mother had whisked her away before she might have said something that would have gotten her punished. However, Frank had never let her forget that. And he never forgot catching Nate comforting her in the barn later that night.

Janice shook her head at the memory. They hadn't even been doing anything. Nate had just held her while she cried and wailed at the injustice. But Frank had assumed the worst. She still cringed in embarrassment, even after all these years. Nate hadn't even looked at her again for six months after the tongue-lashing her father gave him. It had taken Nate almost a year before he had even talked to her alone again.

Now that she was back on the Three Sisters Ranch and Nate was irreplaceable because of the work he'd taken over because her father was sick, old habits were still hard to break. Janice had to remind herself that she didn't have to apologize for talking with Nate or what her father called "taking Nate away from his duties." And Nate could tell her father to jump in a lake. Frank relied on him too much to fire him.

Of course, there was precedent to Frank flying off the handle and kicking people off the ranch. When her sister Kelly had been pregnant and refused to tell her parents who the father was, her father told her to either spill the beans or he'd throw her out.

Kelly had left the next morning.

So Janice could see the benefit of walking on eggshells around her father, even though he and Kelly had reconciled after Alissa was born five years ago.

A squeaky, creaking noise broke Janice out of her brooding thoughts. She looked up to see her sister Emily dragging a wagon full of boxes her way.

"Come on and help me decorate the barn," Emily said, holding up a long strand of pine garland twisted in lights. Christmas was Emily's favorite holiday. She loved the decorations and the colored lights. And, of course, the presents.

"Where did you dig all these up?" Janice asked, poking through the dusty boxes.

"All over. Most of the stuff was crammed in the attic behind Aunt Candace's chests."

Shaking a wreath that was decorated with tequila bottle nips and mini cowboy boots, Janice could see why they had been stuffed away out of sight. "I think I'll bring this over to the bunkhouse. The boys should get a kick out of it." It would make a nice peace offering to Nate, as well. She should go over and apologize for bawling like a lost calf.

Later, though. Let him cool down a bit. He was a lot like her father in the temper department sometimes.

As she helped Emily nail up the garland over the outside of the barn, Janice asked, "What's Donovan been up to?"

"Don't ask." Emily made a face.

Donovan Link was her parents' other tenant. He was a hunter and paid them a great deal of money each month to run a Texan safari in their unused pastures where feral hogs, deer, and elk ran wild. He was also Emily's fiancé, which was pretty amusing since she was a strict vegetarian and animal rights activist. Emily's reaction to the question meant Donovan was either culling the feral hogs or something along those lines.

"How did your client meeting go?" Emily sat down on a sawhorse and began to untangle a string of lights.

"Don't ask," Janice said, dejected again. There was a better chance of it snowing in Texas this Christmas than her getting anyone to book a retreat.

"You'll get some people answering your ads soon."

Emily was born optimistic.

The construction on the retreat center was finally complete, but it remained empty. It was a rustic four-bedroom meeting house with a full kitchen and a communal bathroom. It wasn't a luxury spa by any stretch of the imagination, and maybe that was why she was having trouble getting guests to sign up for her enrichment programs. She had put flyers up around town, placed ads online and in local newspapers about animal therapy and team-building exercises centered on ranch life. She had hoped to attract women looking to improve themselves—or at least their outlook. But so far there hadn't been the slightest bit of interest.

"I've got an idea," Emily said. "Put some of the ranch hands on the ads. Have them take off their shirts and look all sweaty and dusty."

"It's not that kind of retreat."

"Maybe you need to change your business plan, then."

Janice chucked a plastic angel ornament at her head. It missed by a mile.

"Or at least, add a hot tub."

Unfortunately, Janice's bank loan hadn't been enough to give the place more spit and polish. Hot tub aside, she would have liked everyone to at least have their own bathroom. But that would have put her way over budget, and since her two pride-and-joy horses were collateral, she wouldn't dare spend a penny more than was necessary. As it was, she was going to have to scramble to pay her loan installment next month. There was simply no money coming in. She had been devoting most of her time to making sure the retreat center was welcoming, homey, and comfortable. When she wasn't agonizing over candles and programming, she was trying her hand at social media marketing and advertisement. Anything to get the word out there.

But the only nibble she had received was from Mr. Grabass and that wasn't even what she was trying to accomplish here. Still, it had been money and she was grateful that her father was talking her up to his friends—even if it had nothing to do with her retreat.

At this point, maybe she should look into giving horse-back-riding lessons. Hell, maybe she should advertise dressage lessons. Lord knew her horses could use the exercise.

Speaking of the horses, she should check on them while she was here. They were sensitive and if they had heard her crying, they would need to be soothed a bit. Leaving Emily sorting out glass baubles, Janice went over to Black Dahlia's stall. She stroked the Andalusian's neck and wished she was back home in Kentucky. No, that wasn't quite true. She wished her family's ranch wasn't on the verge of bankruptcy. She wished she didn't have to risk her horses for the bank loan. She wished someone would sign up for a retreat. She wished for a lot of things, actually.

"Wish in one hand, crap in the other. See which gets filled up first," Janice quoted her father's favorite expression.

Emily snorted with laughter and Janice realized she'd spoken aloud.

"Ain't that the truth," Emily said. "I'm going to decorate the bushes out front with the lights. Want to help?"

"I'll catch up with you. I've got a few things to do here."

"Make sure you keep the dogs out of Dad's way. Bowser ate his slipper."

"Oh no," Janice groaned. "Is he okay?"

"Bowser puked it back up, but Dad's not too happy with

him."

"I'll keep Bowser with me tonight."

Her mother loved the rescue beagle that Janice had brought back from Kentucky, but he and his other five siblings needed a little more training before they could settle into the routine of the ranch. Usually, Janice gave them the run of the retreat center since she'd been sleeping there. But once she had clients, the dogs would have to come back to her parents' house with her and stay there for the duration of the retreat. Janice had been getting them slowly used to the idea—the dogs and her parents both.

Moving on to Synergy, her thoroughbred who had never won a race, Janice offered him a peppermint and he took it greedily. "Just one," she said. Any more than that and he wouldn't eat anything else all day. She'd paid way too much for him, but she hated his owner. He had been too quick to discipline and if Janice had heard him threaten Synergy with the "glue factory" one more time, she would have taken the riding crop and beat *his* flank with it to see how he liked it.

Synergy needed to run. He had a lot of energy and would act out if he didn't get to gallop pell-mell to dispel some of it. And if Janice was honest with herself, she adored racing him along a tract of land. It was the polar opposite of the controlled dressage that Black Dahlia could perform—when the mood struck her. The problem was with all the new construction going on with Kelly and her fiancé Trent's house being built and Emily's wind farm plans, there wasn't a safe stretch of land to ride Synergy full out. There was too much overgrowth and ruts to risk it.

If they still had the dressage ring she'd made her father build for her when she was growing up, at least she could ride him around there. But Frank had plowed over it once she had left the ranch to work in Kentucky. Maybe, she could ask Trent to put his bulls into the holding pens while she rode Synergy around in a circle, but she didn't want to disrupt his business.

"I'll be back later," she promised Synergy. If he behaved, Janice could ride him to one of the unused pastures and let him have his head. It wasn't like she was doing anything else.

Picking up the wreath, she headed to the bunkhouse where the ranch hands were having dinner. Nate was on the porch talking with the guys, probably going over tomorrow's plans. He pointedly ignored her as she hung up the wreath on the door. A couple of the guys said hello to her, but snapped back to attention at Nate's glare. Janice waited until he was done talking with them, and then caught up to him as he walked back to his small cottage.

"Hey, wait up," she called, jogging toward him.

"If you're here to continue to read me the riot act, you can save your breath." He waved his hand at her.

"I'm not." She followed him up the small stairs to his porch. "I wanted to thank you for your concern." *Even though it was unnecessary and high-handed*, she added to herself.

He crossed his arms over his wide chest and glared down at her as if he'd heard the last part. "You didn't have to come all this way for that. What do you want?"

She fought the urge to slug him in the arm. "I didn't

want you to think I was ungrateful and I felt bad about losing my shit. It's not you. It's everything." Janice sagged against the porch railing. "I'm worried I'm going to lose my horses." To her horror, her voice wavered. Damn it, she was not going to cry in front of Nate again. She was tougher than that, but lately...

"It's been a rough couple of months," Nate agreed.

It was uncanny that he picked up on things she didn't say. Emily often joked that Nate and Janice could have entire conversations with each other without saying a word. It was true, too.

Janice nodded and then walked over to Nate and untangled his arms. She stepped closer and wrapped her arms around his chest.

"Janice," he choked out.

She was too used to him to try and argue. "Just give me a minute."

Resting her cheek against his chest, Janice breathed in and was comforted by his strong, sturdy presence.

"It'll all work out," he said gruffly.

"I don't see how," she said, her voice muffled by his shirt. Janice wished he wouldn't talk. Kelly had Trent. Emily had Donovan. It made her heart hurt that she couldn't have Nate. If he just held her, she could lapse into the fantasy that he was as wildly in love with her as she was with him. And if he spoke, she was brought back to the reality that in a few seconds, he would literally put her at arm's length.

If he hadn't snuck a few kisses in over the years, Janice would have gotten the message that he wasn't interested.

What killed her was that he was. He told her time and time again that he didn't want to act on their mutual attraction for each other out of respect for her father. First, it had been because they were too young. Then, it had been the distance between them. But they weren't kids anymore. They were adults. Janice just wanted to explore the forbidden passion so obviously there. Would it fizzle out after they indulged in it, or would it grow stronger?

She was at the ranch to stay and so was he—as long as they could keep from declaring bankruptcy. Janice was tired of tiptoeing around her feelings. She was fed up of being in limbo. It was time to cowboy up. If this wasn't meant to be, then so be it. But she had to try. She had to take the risk. If he didn't feel the same way, then it was time to put on her big girl panties and move on.

"I'm afraid of failing," Janice admitted. If they lost the ranch, she'd lose Nate too.

"You cast your line. Now, you just have to wait for the fish to bite," he said.

She hated fishing. It was boring. It made her twitchy to sit and wait when she could be out there doing something. But everyone else seemed to love it, so she went along with it. And it was one of her retreat selections, so Janice needed to get used to it.

"I should go," she said, not moving.

"Mmm." He stroked her hair.

She'd had it cut short in Kentucky, but when she came back and saw Kelly's long strawberry-blonde hair, Janice had regretted it. But now with Nate running his fingers through it, she was glad not to have any snarls to break the moment.

Loud shotgun blasts startled her out of his arms. "That was damned closer than it should have been," Janice said.

"Whitetails have been a pain in the ass lately." Nate stepped back from her, and she wrapped her arms around herself, suddenly cold. The evenings were getting crisp and chilly. She should have worn a sweater, but she had wanted to look professional for Mr. Slapass.

"I'm going to give Donovan a piece of my mind," Janice said, scowling off into the distance where the shots had come from. "If I had been on Synergy, he would have spooked."

She didn't mind the whitetail deer so much, although they drove her mother crazy when they ate her strawberries. The feral hogs, on the other hand, were getting bold. Still, she hated hearing gunshots so close to their houses…though it was better than being surprised by one of the nasty alpha boars. Her dogs would go crazy and confront the hog and it would end horribly because most of her dogs were all bark and no bite. The hogs on the other hand were crazy and mean, with vicious tusks. They moved faster than anything that size should be able to.

Nate rolled his eyes. "That horse is dangerous."

"He is not," she scoffed. "He's just high-strung."

"Both your horses are. Overbred, fancy, spoiled—"

She held up her palm. "Stop trying to start a fight. I'm going."

"I wasn't trying to kick you out," he drawled with a slight flush to his high cheekbones.

Yes, he had been. But Janice wasn't going to call him on

it. She had something better in mind for him. It was time Nate got a taste of his own medicine when it came to kissing and running. "Anyway, I've got to get back. I promised Kelly I'd babysit Alissa so she and Trent could have a date night."

Alissa was five, and Janice was teaching her how to play gin rummy so they could team up and beat MeMaw and PawPaw.

"Date night?" Nate rolled his eyes. "Why don't they just wait until she's in bed?"

This time she did slug him. "Because sometimes it's fun to go out to dinner and see a movie. It's called romance. You should try it some time."

"I don't have time for that. I've got to be up before dawn."

"Sleep is overrated," she said, and before she could lose her nerve, she stepped in and kissed him.

She had meant it to be just a quick smack on the lips, like the kisses he gave her on the infrequent times he felt the need. Except, his mouth was hot and tasted sweet. Janice melted against him and licked his lips until they parted for her tongue. Then all hell broke loose as he hauled her up tight and pressed her against the side of the cottage.

Damn.

Reason and good sense fled hand in hand. Janice gripped his shirt so tight, two buttons flew off. Nate turned her sweet and sassy kiss into an inferno and she could barely hold on to her intentions when he ran his hands all over her body.

The shotguns went off again and they jumped apart so fast, Janice almost fell. Nate caught her and dragged her back against him.

"What the hell was that about?" he growled, his voice uneven and his breath ragged.

"Seemed like the thing to do," she said, licking her swollen lips. Janice already missed his mouth on hers.

"Don't complicate things," Nate said.

She pushed out of his arms. She was getting tired of hearing the same old shit.

It felt good to walk away from him for once.

Chapter Three

J ANICE SULLIVAN WAS trouble. Nate knew that from the moment he laid eyes on her ten years ago. She wasn't the gorgeous rodeo queen that her middle sister was or the impishly cute devil their younger sister was. Janice Sullivan was a force of freaking nature. And she fascinated him to the point of obsession.

He had a ton of stuff to do today and none of it had to do with her or her retreat center. And he was so bone-weary tired, he could fall asleep in his saddle if he wasn't careful. If he was smart, he'd nod politely at her and go about his business. He must be a dumb son of a bitch because all he could do was watch the sweet curve of her ass in those jeans. She turned toward him, catching him looking at her, and something in his eyes made her drop the half-full bag of feed she was carrying. Blushing, she then bent over to pick it up and he could see halfway down her blouse.

Have mercy.

She had rocked his world last night with that kiss that kept him up half the night thinking about it. Four a.m. had come early and even the thermos of black coffee at his side didn't make any promises of keeping him from yawning in the saddle. He wasn't sure why Janice was up so early. A part of him hoped she was riding out with them today. But Frank hadn't mentioned it. All his daughters could rope an errant cow and hold their own out on the trail. The youngest, Emily, was training to take over the ranch from Frank one day. But only Janice distracted him while they were on the job.

Nate had expected to feel conflicted when Janice had come home to help her parents. But he wasn't. Not at all. He wanted to make Janice Sullivan his.

Unfortunately, he'd promised her father he wouldn't.

When Janice had announced her plans for her "boohoo club" as Frank called it, Frank took Nate aside for a little talk. Nate had been prepared to politely, but very firmly tell him to shove it up his ass if Frank tried to warn him away from his daughter again. They weren't kids anymore and Nate had waited for her to find herself in Kentucky and then come to her damned senses and come back here where she belonged.

For years, it had seemed like that wasn't going to happen, but when Frank sent out his distress call, Janice came home and was setting down roots.

About damned time.

That meant she was going to stay, and since he wasn't going anywhere, it would be the perfect time for them to finally explore the chemistry or whatever the hell it was between them. Unfortunately, for the first time in his damned life, Frank had asked for something instead of demanding it.

It wasn't any surprise that the old man was slowing down. The first heart attack was the beginning of the end of Frank's career. Nate saw him every day and saw the pain that he was in. Pain made Frank meaner than usual because he was frustrated and worried sick about his daughters and his ranch. The second heart attack had almost killed him. And he still wasn't one hundred percent back to normal. Nate wondered if this was Frank's new normal and felt a stab of pity for the man who had always been larger than life.

"You know you're the son I never had," Frank had said, which right there had taken the legs out from under Nate. Because he had been the father that Nate wished he'd had instead of the hard-drinking, fist-swinging gambler who had orphaned him when he had been a kid.

"I don't have a lot more years left in me."

"Don't talk crap," Nate had growled at him, fear making him just as mean as Frank could be.

"We may have to sell the ranch. You need to prepare for that. Unless one of the girls marries smart. It's not going to be Kelly. She's got to marry a good daddy for Alissa. And it's not going to be Emily because…" Frank had rolled his eyes. "She doesn't have the temperament for settling down with a good match. Janice, though, as long as she has her animals, she's happy. She's the smart one."

Nate thought his jaw would crack from clenching it so hard. All their lives, Frank had referred to Kelly as the pretty one, Janice as the smart one and Emily as the baby. For the most part, they hadn't let that define them. But it still pissed him off to hear it. All the sisters were smart, pretty, hard-working and loyal to their family. "You underestimate them. You always have," he had told Frank.

"Don't tell me about my daughters," Frank had snapped back with his usual snarl. But then he'd sagged, as if that little bit of anger had taken too much out of him. "I'm asking you to be a gentleman and step away from Janice. You're a good friend to her and to me. But you can't make her happy. You're too much like me. Impatient and gruff. She needs someone more suited to her. She's sensitive."

About as sensitive as a rattlesnake after you stepped on it, but Nate had kept that to himself. "I think you should let her decide that," he had said instead.

"I've got a better idea." Frank had chuckled.

Frank wanted her to marry Pete Dickerson, their veterinarian. And while Nate knew that Janice would balk at any hint of an arranged marriage, he had to admit that her and Pete made a good couple. She certainly deserved a doctor for a husband rather than a ranch foreman, especially since Doc Pete was rich. As in filthy rich. As in he didn't need to work. He just did it because he loved animals. Which made it difficult to hate the son of a bitch.

And for all the sisters' good intentions, the only thing that could save the Three Sisters Ranch was the type of money Pete could bring to the table. Nate couldn't compete. And he loved the Sullivan family too much to disrespect them by ruining this opportunity to save the ranch.

They had lucked out when Kelly hooked up with PBR star Trent Campbell. His purse winnings saved them from immediate bankruptcy. But Emily was looking to spend money before she made any, using part of the ranch as a wind farm. Trent had given her a loan to get her started, but the wind turbines were expensive, and she could only buy a few of them. It would be a while before they were up and running and then a year or two, at least, before they were profitable. As far as her marrying rich, her fiancé Donovan was scraping by just like the rest of them.

So that left Janice and rich Doc Pete. If Janice wanted Pete, Nate would step aside. It would kill him to do it, but he would.

Nate shook his head and whistled for Daisy, his Australian shepherd. He wasn't expecting a pack of mutts thundering over to him. "No," he said. "Shoo."

But Daisy brought her six friends, Janice's dogs that she had rescued from a kill shelter in Kentucky. Knowing Janice, he supposed he should be happy it was only six. Daisy was a cow dog through and through, and took great pleasure in herding. Cows. People. Other dogs. Didn't matter. She'd tried herding the barn kittens once and gotten her nose smacked for her trouble by the mama kitty.

"Janice," he hollered. The last thing he had wanted was to be up close and personal with her this morning, especially since her father would be riding the range with them today. Nate swore that man had a second sense about Nate and Janice being alone together. Fortunately, Frank no longer tried to be in the saddle. He used the truck and oversaw moving the cattle to the new pasture from the comfort of his ancient Ford F-150. But if he saw them standing close, Nate wouldn't hear the end of it.

"Stop yelling," she said, coming over. "I'm right here." Her voice was loud in the predawn and she wrapped her sweater around her tighter.

"Where's your jacket?"

"In the small barn. A few of the horses have ringworm and we've isolated them."

"We?" Nate said as Daisy and her pack circled around him and Janice.

"Pete is coming back later, but I wanted to make sure the horses were comfortable. I'm going back to bed." She stifled a yawn.

Nate's gut clenched. Good ole Doc Pete. He wondered if she had thought about their kiss at all or if she and Pete had been too busy. "Good," he forced himself to say. "Take these idjits with you before they get stomped on."

"Daisy wouldn't let that happen." Janice crouched down and was immediately assaulted by ecstatic tail-wagging dogs. And Nate could see down her damned shirt again. He was fascinated by the sprinkle of freckles over her cleavage. A few years ago, he couldn't get out of the pond after seeing them peeking out of her bathing suit. He had been rock hard with no chance of it going down until the water got chilly.

"Do me a favor anyway, and keep them with you." Nate forced himself to look at the mutts instead of the curve of her breasts. "I might have use for the shepherd mix if he can be trained. But not today. I'm short men and I can't take the time to watch him."

"Why are you short staffed?"

"We had to let ten guys go. Can't afford to pay them."

Janice closed her eyes and shook her head. "Damn. Right before Christmas."

"I know. We gave them a bonus. What little we could."

"Was it because we sold a hundred heads at auction last month?"

"Partly. We just need to run leaner than we have been."

Biting her lip, Janice ruffled a husky mix behind the ears. Nate couldn't keep all their names straight. Although the beagle carrying a mangled slipper was Bowser—or *goddammit Bowser* as Frank liked to call him. "I could ride out if you needed a hand."

Nate was tempted, but last night's kiss and the feel of her against him were forefront in his mind. "No, stay with the sick horses."

"Doc Pete can handle them," she said. "He's got a way with animals."

Doc Pete could kiss his ass.

"You want to help? Keep your dogs from following us." Nate turned on his heel and walked back to large barn, where his horse, Jonas, was waiting for him and Daisy to lead the team out. He knew he had been abrupt, but the longer he stood there talking with her, the more he would want to ask her to ride out with them. He loved riding with her— when she took a sensible trail horse instead of one of her two prima donnas.

Frank would catch up with them in the truck in about an hour. Or maybe he wouldn't. Nate hoped he'd take it easy and rest, but easy wasn't in Frank's wheelhouse. Hell, it wasn't in Nate's either. And if he was lucky, Doc Pete would be gone by the time they got back. If he was even luckier, Pete would do something to piss Janice off.

"The boys all pitched in. We've got about three hundred dollars to buy toys for the firefighters' toy drive," Esteban, his assistant foreman, said to him as they rode out in the predawn light. It was a beautiful morning and Nate hoped that the weather held. They had a lot of things to do and rain would just slow them down.

"I'll ask Donovan and Trent if either of them is interested in matching that. Then we'll be in good shape." Nate might be able to scrape some more together, too.

"Hell, if Donovan returns all the empties from his old hunting parties, that should bring in a few more bucks."

Nate smirked. Those hunters had drunk more than they hunted, but as long as they paid for the experience, who was he to judge?

"You got plans for Christmas?"

"Nah." Nate didn't have any family. If it wasn't for the Sullivans, he would have just gone from ranch to ranch working wherever they needed an extra hand.

"You?"

"Yeah, going to go see my mom and brothers. They're traveling up here to Last Stand. They've heard so much about it from me blabbering on, they wanted to see it."

"Bring 'em by. We'll give them the dollar tour."

Esteban reminded Nate a lot of himself when he was young. They both had shitty fathers. They'd both grown up having shitty Christmases. And this ranch had helped save them both.

Nate had wound up at the Three Sisters Ranch after his father's death. A vicious drunk who liked to use his fists, Nate's father was bound to die young. He had died after his horse threw him. He had been drinking and was too rough on the horse. It bucked him off, and he slammed his head on a rock. They said he died instantly, which was a better end than the son of a bitch deserved.

Nate had been sixteen and after wandering around taking the odd ranch job here and there, he'd seen a flyer that the Three Sisters Ranch was hiring. Frank Sullivan had made him go to high school and get his diploma, but allowed him to live in the bunkhouse with the ranch hands. Nate worked on the ranch before and after school, and had felt damned lucky for the privilege.

And his Christmases had gotten much better, too. The ranch hands always did secret Santa gifts and the Sullivan family catered a big spread for them on Christmas Eve. After Nate graduated high school and was working on the ranch full-time, they'd invite Nate over for Christmas Day and it was almost like having a family, especially when he could have a few moments alone with Janice. Sometimes, he wondered when they were going to wake up and realize he wasn't family. He was just the foreman and maybe one day they wouldn't need him anymore. Hell, one day he might take a bad toss from a horse like his old man did. Of course, with his luck, Nate would live and then what would he do? Where would he go? Nate sighed. He hated this time of the year. His mind always asked stupid-ass questions like that during the holidays. Best to just ignore them and get on with work.

"I heard that the Daughters of Last Stand were going to put up an angel tree in the library with requests from the kids as ornaments. We should take a ride next week and see if we can get something for the older kids, the teenagers."

He and Esteban exchanged a grim look, but didn't say anything further on the subject. That's what he liked about the younger man. He didn't fill up silence with stuff that didn't need to be said.

"My two brothers are looking for work. Any chance there might be some openings in the new year?"

Nate shook his head regretfully. "I don't think so."

Esteban nodded. "Yeah, I figured. But maybe there'll be a Christmas miracle or something."

And that was the difference between Esteban and him. Esteban still believed in shit like that.

"Christmas is just another day."

"Whatever you say, Ebenezer Scrooge."

"Bah humbug. Quit jabbering at me and go catch that calf." Nate jerked his chin at a longhorn baby making a run for it.

Chapter Four

JANICE'S FATHER PULLED up in his truck and rolled down the window. "You want a ride?"

Frank Sullivan looked tired, but determined. Janice wished he'd let Nate and the boys take care of things. She'd much rather have her father tooling around the ranch on the Gator and doing chores closer to the ranch house.

"No," she said, leaning on the door of the truck. "I'm going to take a nap until Pete gets here."

"That was a good catch on the ringworm. We could have had an epidemic if you hadn't quarantined them when you did."

"I'm just glad I noticed it," she said. She had been helping brush some of the work horses when she noticed some patchy spots.

"You should go out on the trail tomorrow. I want you to take a look at the stock."

"You should get Pete to go," she said, stifling a yawn. The real reason she was up so early was her lovesick heart wanted to see Nate this morning and try to work out if the kiss had affected him the same way it had her. Well, she got her answer. A big fat no.

"Can't afford Pete to do any more than he's been doing. Put that vet tech degree I paid for to good use, and get your ass out there tomorrow."

"You want me to earn my keep?" she asked bitterly. The next thing he'd start up with was how she should go back to school to become a veterinarian like Doc Pete. And it didn't matter that she had told him countless times that she didn't want to. Frank Sullivan heard what he wanted to hear. And he wanted to hear that she was a veterinarian.

"It's a damn sight better than running a hand-holding cult for cowgirl wannabes."

Janice held on to her temper only because she was too tired to fight with him. "I've been keeping busy checking on the heifers. You're going to need to get some more feed."

"Already?" Frank sighed.

"About a ton should get us through the end of the year."

"All right. Tell your mother to place the order and I'll send Nate tonight to pick it up. We paid last month's bill, right?"

"Yeah, Dad. We did."

"That's a relief."

It was. Janice knew, though, that they would go hungry before the cattle did. Luckily, the corn, oats, and barley just supplemented the hay and what they got grazing the pasture. Still the new mothers and babies would need more than what they usually went through because of the overgrazed pastures.

Patting the truck door, she said, "I'll help Mom and stay to look the cows over when we bring lunch this afternoon in the chuck wagon."

The chuck wagon was a pickup truck that held a pop-up canopy, tables, chairs and coolers of food and beverages for the ranch hands when they were out deep and working through the lunch hour. Her mother was doing some extra baking for the Last Stand Christmas tree lighting and the parade this week, and Janice and her sisters were chipping in wherever they could.

"Good girl," her father grunted and took off in a cloud of dust.

She found her mother feeding the chickens and geese, a basket of eggs next to her. "Can you check everyone's water?" Sarah Sullivan asked, stretching with her hand on her back. "Emily is on the tractor right now baling hay, but I want to get that done before we hit the kitchen."

Emily was in training to take over the running of the ranch from her father. And all Janice could say to that was *better you than me.* Her father wasn't letting go of the reins of the ranch anytime soon, but that did give Emily a large learning curve to become an expert on the things she pretty much had done all her life. She was probably tickled to be on the tractor and Janice was willing to bet if her father knew she was, he wouldn't be in such a hurry to join Nate in the pastures.

"Sure." Janice nodded, but she didn't move. "Mom, what are you and Dad going to do if we have to sell?"

It was the first time any of them had dared to broach the subject with them, but Janice was worried that they might not be able to keep the creditors at bay.

"Oh, I don't know. I always wanted to live by the ocean. Maybe we'd go out to California."

Janice couldn't picture her father on the West Coast. "Maybe Florida?"

Sarah shrugged. "I guess it also depends on where you girls are. Kelly and Alissa will be here. Donovan's business is doing all right, so he and Emily will stay as long as the new owner continues to lease the property to them. I imagine the question you really want to know the answer to is, what are you going to do, isn't it?"

As usual, her mother saw right through her. "I guess it would be back to Kentucky for me."

"Do you have someone there?"

"I've got friends, and Kentucky Dressage would take me back in a heartbeat." They had been sad to see her go.

"Wouldn't you want to stay in Texas, close to your sisters?"

"Kentucky isn't that far away." But in her heart of hearts, Janice didn't want to go. She had missed Last Stand. Maybe ranching wasn't the life for her, but there was a veterinary hospital in town that could possibly need another technician. She'd hate it, but she needed the money a steady job would give her. At least she'd put her degree to good use and get her father off her back. "Then again, maybe Pete Dickerson might need some help."

Her mother frowned. "You'd be traveling all over hell and creation. Why don't you go work for Honeyman Veterinarian Hospital? I called Miles because everyone knows he's trying to get his sister Mia to work for him. I figured he might be able to give you a few hours."

"Mom," she groaned. "I don't need you to find me a job."

"You should ask him today," her mother said, pretending she didn't hear Janice's protest. "I know you're worried about paying your loan. With a steady job, it would take some of the pressure off."

Janice nodded. It would be the smart thing to do, especially since her women's retreat business seemed to be a bust. Or at the very least, slow to launch. Even though it wouldn't pay much, she needed to start generating some extra cash quickly. "I'll talk to him. If he doesn't need someone, maybe he knows someone who does."

She took the Gator around to the gated pastures and made sure everyone had food and water, and by the time she got back, she saw Pete's truck outside of the barn where they had isolated the horses with ringworm. So much for her nap. But then again if she could make things easier on her father and mother, it was worth losing some sleep.

"Hey, Pete," she said, walking into the barn. It had a strong smell of disinfectant and she wrinkled her nose.

He was in a stall with one of the horses. "Glad you're here. Can you hold him while I give him the antibiotic?"

"Sure thing." Janice moved in and took the reins that he had put on the horse to keep it steady while he examined it.

"You did a good job clipping the area," he said.

"Thanks. I put an anti-fungal patch on."

"I saw that. Good work. I'm going to write you a prescription for Nolvasan, though. You're going to need something stronger for this one. He's got an infection."

"I thought so, but I was hoping to treat it with over-the-counter medication."

"You've got good instincts. You should go back to school and become a full-fledged vet." He patted the horse and took off the reins. After leaving the stall, he washed his hands in hot soapy water before moving on to the next horse.

"Yeah, maybe someday when money isn't so tight." She smiled a bit sadly at him.

Pete flushed and looked down. "I thought the ranch was doing better. Trent seems to be doing great."

Janice plastered a smile on her face. The last thing she wanted was people to start talking about their finances any more than they probably were. That was one curse of being in a small town like Last Stand. "You know how it is. We have our ups and downs."

She was about to swallow her pride and ask him for a job when he said, "I was talking with Rita Alvarez the other day. Have you met her? She's a therapist who works out of Jameson."

"You okay, Doc?" she asked, opening the stall door for him to look at the next horse. Jameson was the local hospital.

"Me? Oh yeah." He cleared his throat. "We were in the library when we ran into each other, not the hospital."

"Oh," Janice said, smiling. Pete was blushing. Maybe he had a crush on the therapist.

"I was telling her about your retreat center and she seemed really excited."

"You did?" She could kiss Pete. This was one of the benefits about being in a small town where everyone knew your business. Like the fertilizer they used, networking was organic and plentiful. "Thank you so much."

"I have her card somewhere. Maybe in the truck. You should call her and get together. I think you could help each other out. She has a lot of clients and maybe the two of you can put together a retreat or something for them?"

"I will. I'll definitely call her. I don't know what to say. I've been so discouraged lately about getting started. You've made my whole week with this."

"Good." He gave her a quick nod and got back to work. By the time he was finished, all the horses in the small barn checked out with just mild cases of ringworm, with the exception of his first patient, who had it the worst.

"I should give the rest of them a look over."

"The majority are still out with the ranch hands. I'll check them out tonight and if I run into something I can't handle, I'll give you a call." Janice walked him back to his truck.

"Let me see if I can find Rita's card for you." He shuffled through his glove compartment and then his jacket. "It must be in my other coat. I hope I didn't send it through the wash."

"Don't worry about it. I'll track her down through the hospital. Thanks again."

"Anytime." He waved as he drove off.

After heading into the ranch house, she helped her mother with lunch. When the meatballs were baking in the oven, she went into the office to locate a contact number for

Rita Alvarez.

She found a number for her at the hospital and after a few transfers, left a message for her to call her back on her cell phone. It would be great if Rita could refer people to Janice's retreat center. If not, maybe she'd let Janice drop off some flyers for her office.

Then it was back in the kitchen to bake several trays of brownies for dessert. In another hour, she would drive out to the pasture with her mother and serve lunch to the crew. Janice took the time to face-plant on her bed to recharge.

Of course, as she was dozing off, her cell phone rang. Fumbling with it, she rolled over and was glad that it wasn't a video call. "Hi," she answered.

"Janice Sullivan?" a warm voice asked.

"Yes. Rita?"

"That's me. Pete Dickerson spoke so highly of you. I feel I know you already."

"That was kind of him." Janice sat up in bed and straightened her clothes.

"I was wondering if you could meet for lunch today?"

"Today?" Janice thought about her promise to her father and figured that she could make it up to him by riding out with the boys in the morning. "Sure, what time?"

"Let's meet in an hour at The Hut."

"Sounds good."

Janice took the fastest shower of her life and changed into the suit she had worn when she and Kelly met with the bankers. She hurried down the stairs and asked her mother, "How do I look?"

"You're a little overdressed for the cows," Sarah said wryly.

"Can I have some lipstick?" Alissa asked.

"And a spritz of perfume." She dabbed a bit of color on her niece's lips and sprayed her perfume in front of Alissa. "Now walk through it."

Alissa hopped in and out of it.

"I've got a business meeting. Can I take your car?" she asked her sister Kelly who was taste-testing a meatball before stuffing the submarine-shaped rolls with them.

"I guess," she said. "Keys are in my purse. Does that mean I'm riding out with Mom to serve lunch?"

"Do you mind?" she asked.

"I was going to do it anyway." Kelly waved her hand dismissively.

"Thanks!"

It felt good to get off the ranch for a bit. For all its wide-open spaces, it was a bit claustrophobic with all the expectations and obligations. Still, Janice loved it and didn't want to see the bank sell it off to the highest bidder.

As Janice drove through town, she made sure to give the tour buses a wide berth. After the horrific accident that had happened earlier this year, she was hyper aware of the traffic now. The tourists loved the historical feel of the town and the cute, modern shops. With the town all decked out for Christmas, it was even prettier.

The tree in front of the library had several men in ladders stringing the lights and decorations. She couldn't wait for the parade and the lighting ceremony. She had missed the Last

Stand Rodeo on Fourth of July weekend because she had been moving from Kentucky. Janice was darned sure she wasn't going to miss another one of Last Stand's traditions.

She waved to a few of her friends from high school and pulled into The Hut's parking lot. The local barbecue joint had the best ribs and Janice had dreamed about them when she had been in Kentucky.

She probably should have rethought the white silk blouse if she was going to get barbecue. Maybe she'd stick with the chicken breast and take home a bunch of sloppy pulled pork sandwiches for dinner to make it up to her father for bailing out on him this afternoon.

Looking around the restaurant, she saw a woman she didn't recognize waving her over. She had long, curly black hair and the most stunning turquoise jewelry Janice had ever seen.

"Rita?" Janice asked, shaking her hand.

"Janice, it's nice to meet you."

They placed their order and Janice resisted the urge to add a margarita. Her nerves hadn't been this bad since she'd waited for Kenny to tell her if the bank would fund her loan. After a cursory glance at the menu, they placed their orders. Rita went for the brisket and Janice almost second-guessed herself because that sounded so darn good. Maybe she'd drag Nate out here to celebrate if this worked out, because there was no way she wouldn't drip barbecue sauce all over her suit if she ordered the ribs.

"Tell me about the retreat center you built. Pete said you had some great ideas."

"That was nice of him." She paused to take a sip of her club soda. Janice figured if she did get sauce on her clothes, the club soda would help take the stain out right away. "It's a four-bedroom, one-bathroom house. There's a kitchen, dining, and living room area."

"Could you double up in the bedrooms?"

"Absolutely." Janice nodded. "Two of the bedrooms have king-size beds and the other two have two twin beds in them."

"Do you have any therapy training?" Rita asked.

"No." She shook her head. "I decided to have a getaway for women who wanted to get back to nature. My program is designed more as a self-help retreat. I would provide horse-back-riding training, camping in the backwoods, show them how to build a fire. Basically, they'd become confident just relying on themselves and the skills they learned. There's even a pond for fishing a short hike away."

"It sounds great. What about the ranching experience?"

"Well." Janice chuckled. "They're welcome to help out on the ranch, but I don't expect anyone wants to pay to shovel out horse barns and collect eggs from the chickens."

"You'd be surprised," Rita said. "I've got a group of women that this would be ideal for. But I was thinking of doing something a little different. Would you be open to a new idea?"

"Of course." At this point, short of Rita mentioning that she wanted to run a brothel out of the retreat center, Janice was going to be all in.

"Have you seen the movie *City Slickers* with Billy Crystal?"

"Oh." Janice thought about it. "I think so. A long time ago. On television. Maybe." Suddenly, she had a bad feeling about this idea.

"My group is looking for team-building exercises and one of the things they mentioned was riding out with some cowboys on a cattle drive. This is something your ranch does, right?"

"Well, yes. We do herd the cows to new areas when they've grazed one area too long. It's not every day, though. There's plenty of heifers and steers around the ranch if they're looking to feed cows." Oh please, let them just want to pet cows and pretend to be cowgirls. Her family would never let her live this down.

"It's more than that. They're looking to be a part of something larger."

Wait. That sounded a lot like what she wanted her retreat to be. "They want a sense of accomplishment," Janice added, filling in the blanks. "Do they ride?"

"Most of them do."

"Most?"

"Of the six women who wanted to do this, only two of them have never been on a horse before."

Janice grimaced. "Those women do not want to spend all day in the saddle."

"I was hoping to book the retreat center for two weeks. During that two weeks, they could build up their skills and end their adventure by driving cattle for one day. Is this something you could provide? Of course," Rita added, hurrying on before Janice could say anything, "I wouldn't leave all the programming up to you. These women would have therapy sessions, both group and individual, with me throughout the two weeks. Plus we could throw in some fun activities around town, like the tree lighting and the market."

Janice's heartbeat quickened. She wasn't sure how she was going to convince her father, let alone Nate, to get this to happen. But she knew that she was going to have to try. "I think the Three Sisters Ranch can accommodate you and your group for two weeks. What does your budget look like?"

"We were able to secure a few governmental grants." Rita named a figure that would cover their feed bill for half a year, and keep her loan payments current during that time. For two weeks' worth of work. Even with feeding the six women three meals a day, the profit made her eyes water.

"When were you looking to start?" Janice asked.

Chapter Five

THE NEXT DAY, Janice headed out to Nate's cottage as soon as she woke up. It was still dark and the chill in the air was a brisk reminder that it was December. Perhaps she should have waited a few more hours to talk to Nate, because when he opened the door to scowl at her, he wasn't completely dressed.

Actually, she thought, she'd timed it perfectly. His sun-bronzed skin was muscled and he had wild stallion tattoos over his large arms. She resisted the urge to whistle. He shrugged a flannel shirt on over his T-shirt and while she missed the ripple of skin, she had to admit he looked just as good with clothes on.

"Have you even been to bed yet?" he asked in a groggy voice.

"Of course, why?"

"Because you're wide awake."

"I was hoping to catch you alone for a few minutes before we got started." She pushed by him into his house. "Is the coffee on? I brought you some blueberry muffins."

"Does a bear shit in the woods?" he grumbled while he took the basket of muffins from her.

"Aren't you all charm and sweetness this morning?" Janice bustled into his small kitchen.

"What do you want, Janice?" Nate asked with his mouth half full. "These are fresh baked."

She poured him a cup of coffee while he chewed at her suspiciously.

"Do you have any cream?"

"Why would I have cream?"

"To put in your coffee."

"Next, you're going to ask me for sugar."

Janice looked into her own cup. "You really drink this stuff straight?"

"Puts hair on your chest." He pointed above the refrigerator. "I should have some powdered creamer up there. And the sugar's in the bowl by the stove."

Janice sniffed the creamer suspiciously, but the expiration date was still good and it was better than drinking the tar that he made black. When her cup was doctored enough to be drinkable, she sat down at the table with him. "Before I start, I want you to know that I've already spoken to my father."

"I knew it. This is going to be bad, isn't it?" he asked, taking his third muffin.

"It's not bad. But," she said, raising her gaze to meet his. She almost flinched from his sardonic glare. Clearing her throat, she looked away. It would have been easier to do this over the phone or, better yet, by text. But Nate didn't do either. "I booked my first retreat. It's for six women."

"Okay," he drawled.

"And the money is going to set us up through next year."

"How long are they staying? You running a hotel now?"

"Just two weeks."

He raised an eyebrow. "Just what kind of business are you running? A meth lab?"

She resisted the urge to chuck a muffin at him. "Pete hooked me up with a therapist in town."

"That was nice of him," Nate said between his teeth.

"It was. Anyway, Rita—the therapist—is doing a team-building exercise that will incorporate a lot of the ideas I had for the retreat. And if this works out well, she'll probably do this program a few times a year."

"Okay," Nate drawled out again slowly. "What's this got to do with me?"

"The women will be joining you on the cattle drive at the end of their stay."

"No."

"Nate…"

"No."

"Listen to me, it's a lot of money."

"It's an insurance nightmare. I can't have a bunch of women who have never worked a ranch before out in the pasture with a bunch of cattle that could crush them like bugs."

"Yes, you can. I have it all figured out."

"Of course, you do. The answer is still no." Nate narrowed his eyes at her. "What did your father say?"

"He said it was up to you."

"That chicken-shit bastard," Nate exclaimed.

"Nate!" In all her years, Janice had never heard Nate say anything like that about her father. He practically hero-worshiped him.

"He didn't want to be the bad guy. He didn't want to tell you no and he didn't want the responsibility of turning down all that money. So, he left it to me." Nate pushed back his chair and drained his coffee in one long gulp. "Forget this. I've got work to do."

Damn it. Janice had to leave her coffee or she was going to spill it all over herself chasing after him. "Can you at least hear me out?" she said, half-running in the dark of the predawn. He stopped suddenly and she almost ran into him.

"Fine. Go ahead."

"Can we go back inside and finish our breakfast?"

"No. You don't get to butter me up with your mother's blueberry muffins. If you were really trying, you would have brought over her chicken and dumplings for dinner."

"I can still do that," Janice said, sensing a weakness. "And apple pie for dessert."

"I'm listening." Nate crossed his arms over his chest.

"Most of the women have ridden a horse before."

"Most?" he choked out, eerily mirroring her own reaction.

"The first week, they'll be learning all about the cattle ranch. We'll have activities ranging from mucking out stalls to roping and riding lessons."

"People are spending their hard-earned money for this?"

"Yes. Pay attention. They'll sign waivers. They'll pass your personal inspection or they will stay home the day of the cattle drive. If they can't rope, they'll herd from the back. They'll be partnered up with experienced ranch hands."

"Now you're delegating my cowboys to this?"

"It's one day, Nate. My sisters will be there too, to lend a hand. Maybe even Donovan and Trent."

"You talked to them about this?"

She bit her lip, wondering whether to lie or not. He knew her too well so she said, "Not yet."

He groaned and threw up his hands.

"I wanted to get you on board with it first. But they'll help out. I know they will."

"Darlin', I have a job to do. And if I don't do it, this entire ranch doesn't work out. I don't care how many rich women who want to be cowgirls you have coming in. What you and your sisters seem to forget is the main purpose of this ranch is raising cattle."

"I haven't forgotten that, but it's not enough anymore."

He took in a sharp breath.

She laid a hand on his forearm. "That has nothing to do with you or the hard work you and your men do. It's just a fact of life. If we want to keep the ranch out of bankruptcy, we need to diversify and it's going to take all of us to compromise."

"You want me to compromise?"

"It's one day. You'll have full authority. If someone is a liability, they stay home." She squeezed his arm. "It's not like it's a spring roundup. It's two weeks in the winter, right before Christmas. And it means a lot of money. It will keep the bank at bay and open up a realm of new possibilities.

Please, Nate. Give it a chance. If it's a disaster—"

"And it's going to be."

"—at least we tried. It's either this or I have to get a job with Pete or another vet in the area and that's just going to piss off my father something fierce."

"Janice, you're killing me here."

"I'm not. I'm really not. It's one day, Nate. You'll have me and my sisters, Trent and Donovan there as well. Please."

"Don't give me the puppy dog eyes."

"You don't have to get me a Christmas present if you say yes," she wheedled.

"I wasn't going to get you one anyway."

Liar. He always got her something for Christmas. And she treasured every little trinket.

"It's just one day. You don't have to be the bad guy. We'll get the money to keep us going another six months, which gives Emily time to get those wind turbines up and running. And I'll bring over chicken and dumplings and apple pie."

"With vanilla ice cream?" he asked.

Holy shit, he was going to say yes. "Anything you want."

"Be careful what you offer." Nate leaned down and kissed her.

Could this day get any better?

She wrapped her arms around his neck and enthusiastically returned it.

"I'm going to regret this," he said, breaking off the kiss.

"You won't. I swear you won't." Janice kissed him again. His mouth was hot and wet and she wanted to jump on him and wrap her legs around him, but he'd probably die of shock.

"Stop that," he said. "Or you're going to have to explain to your father why we're late."

"Can I get a rain check then?" she asked. Her heart was flickering and skipping and she couldn't stop grinning.

"We'll talk over chicken and dumplings," he said. "When does this retreat start?"

"Tomorrow."

Nate swore. "Tomorrow? What if I had said no?"

"I would have figured something else out to do with them." She left it unsaid that she had planned to work on him and wear him down until he had said yes. The cattle drive wasn't for another two weeks.

Squinting his eyes at her, he kissed her again. Janice could get used to this.

"What was that for?" she asked, licking her lips.

"Because I like doing it."

"I like when you kiss me, too. Why don't you do it more often?"

Nate closed his eyes in frustration. "You know why."

"So do you, but it doesn't stop you when the mood strikes."

"My mood strikes a lot more than I act on it."

"Really?" Janice was thrilled. "We need to talk about this."

Swearing, Nate drew her in for another kiss. He was easily the most exciting man she had ever met and kissing him in the predawn light felt magical. Goose bumps rose over her arms. He held her tight against him, one hand on her ass and the other on her back. His mouth ravaged hers and she hung on tight to his shoulders. Janice knew her knees would give out as soon as he stopped, so she held on tight until he tore his mouth away.

"I am not going to be a gentleman if we don't stop," he said, breathing heavily.

"I don't want you to be one. I certainly don't feel like a lady."

Nate pressed his forehead against hers. "You complicate things."

"You don't get to tell me I complicate things when you keep kissing me."

"I can't help myself."

Janice wanted to dance with delight. "Nate, it's time."

"It's past time. I got to get to work." He kissed her again and left her breathless.

"That's not what I meant, cowboy," she said, touching her swollen lips as he walked away. This was it—the last time she was going to let him blow hot or cold. He needed to step up and own this or he needed to get out of her head.

And her heart.

Chapter Six

A LONG DAY in the saddle was made slightly better because Janice was with him. He couldn't stop yawning, though. They fed the cows, fretted about the grass, fixed some fencing and when they saw hog ruts tearing up the pasture, Nate knew he had to get Donovan out there after they moved the cows.

"It's a damned epidemic," Frank said. He wasn't above blowing the truck's horn to encourage the cows to move toward the hay. The grass wasn't enough to feed the cattle completely this winter.

While Janice moved among them, giving the cattle a once-over, Nate saw that Frank was staring at his daughter like a proud papa.

"She knows her stuff," Nate said, handing the old man his Thermos of coffee.

"I'm hoping she goes back to school." Frank poured himself a cup. "If she really wanted to help us out, she'd give up on this boohoo club for rich women and finish her course work to becoming a veterinarian. We'd save a bundle on vet bills."

"I imagine her college would cost as much as Emily's

JAMIE K. SCHMIDT

wind turbines."

"About the same long-term investment though. Of course, if she marries Pete, she can do whatever the hell she wants."

Nate tried not to let it show how much that irked him, but he wasn't above needling Frank about it. "Have you talked to Pete about this?"

"No, I figure I'd let nature take its course, now that she's back and Pete's pretty much here every other week. It's only a matter of time."

He was probably right and that soured Nate's mood a bit. "What's Janice think of him?"

"Everybody loves Pete."

Nate scowled and stared off into the distance. That was true.

"I hear he's going to be at the Greenfield auction next Monday. Why don't you take Janice there with the cow trailer? Push them together a little bit and see if you can get some bargains."

"We shouldn't be buying right now," Nate said. "We've got calves coming and we're shorthanded."

"So just go take a look, then. Have Janice ask Pete some questions. It will get them talking and we might get some free advice out of it."

Nate grunted. "I'll ask her, but I think she's going to be busy with her retreat."

Spluttering, Frank put down his coffee. "Are you out of your damned mind? I figured you'd tell her to go jump in a lake."

"If you wanted her to go jump in a lake, you should have told her. It's a lot of money for two weeks' work, and they're going to be acting like unpaid ranch hands for most of it. In fact, they're paying for the privilege. I think that's a win-win."

And it made him a hero in Janice's eyes, which was worth all sorts of aggravation.

"I think you got sweet-talked." Frank cut him a nasty look.

"Chicken and dumplings might have been mentioned."

"It's a damned fool idea."

Nate shrugged. "Money works for me. If it doesn't work out, we still get paid. Maybe enough for a trailer of cattle."

Frank perked up a bit at that. "It would be nice to get ahead of the bills for once." Then he remembered to be surly. "I'm counting on you not to make this a complete shit show. If these women are one bit not up to snuff, they can ride the chuck wagon."

"I'm on it," Nate said. "Don't worry about anything. Worry more about Emily making hay bale crop circles with the claw."

Frank closed his eyes. "That girl."

Nate thought it had been pretty funny. Of course, she wasn't his boss yet. It was only a matter of time when he'd be out here talking with Emily about ranch decisions instead of Frank. But he didn't want to think about that right now. Not when the December air was crisp, the cows were behaving themselves and Janice was going to be smiling at him on the ride home.

"I wouldn't mind seeing this retreat nonsense fail," Frank muttered.

"It's your ranch she's trying to save," Nate said hotly.

"She should be a vet. Look at her out there with them."

Nate liked to look. Janice pushed her glasses up her nose and stroked the cow's side while she talked to it. She hated when the ranch hands got impatient with them when they didn't go docilely into the pen. "She's too kindhearted."

"She used to be," Frank said. "I think she's grown out of it. I think she sees the reality of our world a bit more now. Cows aren't pets. Too bad Emily doesn't see it that way. If she had it her way, we'd be feeding the feral hogs."

"We are feeding the feral hogs, whether we like it or not."

"But we're also shooting them. Or supposed to be. Make sure Donovan clears them out of our pastures instead of dicking around with white elks and shit in the back forty."

"I will mention it to him later. We'll move the cows to another pasture and hopefully he'll take care of the hogs in this area." Nate was just hoping that the new pasture wasn't overgrazed. If so, Emily was going to be doing a lot more crop circles.

On the way back to the ranch, Janice rode side by side with him. A peaceful feeling came over Nate and everything felt right. With her father taking the side road back to the ranch house, Nate could relax next to her and not have to worry about what Frank would do or say about them being together.

"I saw you and Dad talking before. What's he up to?"

Nate shook his head. "Everything from going to a cattle auction to wanting to hunt the hogs himself. And a little interfering into your life." He should tell her what her dad had in mind for her and Doc Pete. But what if instead of laughing it off, she got that calculating look on her face that said she was considering it? Nate wasn't ready to face that just yet. Maybe Monday he'd have to, but for right now? Right now, it was just the two of them. And he wanted to imagine that the impossible was possible, at least for the duration of the ride back to the ranch.

"A little? He must not be feeling well. Let me guess. He was bitching about the boohoo club."

"No more than usual."

"I hate when he calls it that," she said, gripping her reins tight. "It's condescending and mean all at once. Not to mention passive-aggressive."

"More like aggressive-aggressive."

"Well, that's his way. I don't have to like it, though. So, what's his grand scheme for me now? Let me guess, he wants me to get my DVM?"

Nate nodded. That was a safe enough topic.

"There's a lot of that going around." Janice sighed and wiped her brow. She left a dirt mark across her face and he grinned at the sight of it.

"What do you want to do?" he asked.

"Not to work with the large animals, if I don't have to, but it's what the family needs. It's what this area needs. I ran away from it before because I couldn't take the brutality and the indifference people had to these living creatures. Now that I'm back, I have to face that being a veterinarian might be my role in helping save the ranch from bankruptcy."

He could sense the despair and desperation in her voice. Nate knew she was second-guessing herself, but he wasn't sure she knew that. So, he decided to play devil's advocate.

"Why didn't you do that instead of building the retreat? You got the loan for the building. Why didn't you try for a student loan instead?"

Her back stiffened and her chin came up as she rallied to defend her decision. "The retreat center was quicker. And I liked the idea of ranch living helping people become more confident. I figured I could use my love for animals to get people thinking about their problems differently. I'm no therapist, though. That's Rita's job."

"Would you like to be a therapist?" Nate asked.

Janice shook her head. "I can't take being in a classroom. I want to be outdoors. Or at least, working with animals."

And there it was. Nate knew her heart. And that was it in a nutshell. "Have you told your father that?"

She snorted. "Until I'm blue in the face. He thinks I'm wasting my potential. But when you help people feel good about themselves, it's not a waste. When I worked on the farm in Kentucky, putting in a hard day's work and seeing the effort of my work make a difference, it was fulfilling."

"Why did you leave then?"

"You know why."

"You're father's not so bad. You've just got to stand up to him."

"Tell that to Kelly," she said, with a shake of her head. "I left before he threw me out, too."

Nate took in a deep breath in shock. "He would have never done that to you."

"If he did it to his pregnant daughter, why wouldn't he have done it to me?"

He didn't have an answer to that.

"I was defying him more than Kelly was. I didn't want to work with cattle. It wasn't because I couldn't. I didn't want to. And he would never understand that. Just like he never understood my love for dressage. It's like the ultimate form of meditation."

"You lost me there."

"It's good for the horse. They gain strength and focus, not to mention agility."

"Jonas is all that." He leaned forward and rubbed his horse's neck. "And you don't see him dancing around like a ballerina." Nate tried to joke to bring her out of this dark mood. He wasn't used to seeing her sound so lost.

She gave him serious side eye. "I bet Jonas would do excellent in dressage with the right training."

"Stay away from my horse. You've already got two spoiled brats of your own to play around with."

"Maybe you should try it?"

"Try what?"

"Dressage."

He snorted. "And why would I do that?"

"You can't be a grumpy asshole. The horse senses it and reacts to it. It would be a good discipline for you, too. It will center you and help you calm yourself."

"I like being a grumpy asshole."

"I could tell."

"Calm and centered won't get the cattle to the fields and the ranch hands organized," Nate argued.

"I'm telling you, it helps."

"I believe you." The last thing he wanted to do was get in an argument with her. He liked it when they joked around, but her somber mood just overwhelmed the conversation.

"I needed that centering calm when I was growing up. Hell, even after I finished college. I could have stayed local and worked at Honeyman Veterinarian Hospital," she said. "But that wasn't what Dad wanted. He wanted me here. I wanted to be here, too. I liked ranch life. I was a part of something. If I didn't do my assigned tasks, everyone else's job got harder. Like if the cows didn't get daily water or the eggs didn't get collected."

"Or if a fence was down or a calf got separated from the herd."

"Right." Janice nodded. "What I did mattered. It's hard to feel helpless when you brought a calf back to his mama. Sometimes when I think I'm losing control over everything, I want to ride out and prove to myself that I am a capable adult who can make a difference." She sighed. "I want to give that feeling to other women. Although, I'm not sure what I'm going to do if the ranch goes bankrupt."

"You can't base your self-worth on the ranch," he said.

"I'm not. But sometimes when I forget that I'm strong, doing these little things reminds me. If I feel that way, surely other women do, too. Yeah, my checkbook might not be balanced, but I could catch and cook my own dinner."

Reaching over, he took her hand in his. "You can always come and talk to me. You know that, right?"

She nodded. "I do. I'm sorry for waylaying you before coffee this morning. I just wanted you to see how important this was for me. It's a chance to prove to my dad that I can still be successful, even if I don't follow his plan for me."

Those words stirred him. Pete was her father's plan for her. Would it be possible that if she didn't follow his plan, she would pick Nate? He was willing to wait and see. He dropped her hand before any of the ranch hands decided it would be a good idea to razz him about it. They'd need all their teeth for chewing dinner tonight.

"We're cooking up some steaks tonight. Want to join us?"

"Are you kidding? I'm so hungry I could clear out an all-you-can-eat buffet."

"You should have eaten more at lunch."

"There's only so much chili and corn bread my stomach can stand before revolting."

"Tenderfoot," he scoffed.

"I don't think I'm up for another group meal with the boys, though. Do you want to go out to dinner instead?" she asked.

He did. But her father wouldn't like it. "I'm filthy. I need to take a shower, gulp down a quick steak, and then crash right into bed."

"Take a shower. It will refresh you."

"Refresh?" Nate quirked an eyebrow at her. Cowboys

didn't refresh.

"And then we can go grab a few beers at the Last Stand Saloon."

"I can't take the crowds." The last thing he wanted was to be around a bunch of loud drunks. Nate knew it was irrational, but lately his patience was stretched so thin that even stuff like being around that many people seemed too much to bear. He wondered if he was becoming a hermit. It didn't sound so bad. People left you the hell alone.

Janice frowned at him. "If you don't want to go out, bring some steaks back to your place and we can have a nice quiet dinner together."

That sounded like heaven, but it would get back to her father. "Should we invite your family?" That would be safest. Sarah would probably just invite him over there instead of having the whole crew come to the cottage.

"Hell, no. Mom's got a meeting at the library about the tree-lighting ceremony. Kelly and Trent are doing their thing, and Emily and Donovan are taking my dad out for vegetarian food."

Nate couldn't stop the quick bark of laughter that erupted. "Does Frank know that?"

"I didn't ask. But pasta is vegetarian, so if worse comes to worst, he'll probably load up on the carbs."

Well, if Frank was going to be preoccupied tonight and Janice would be eating all alone anyway, Frank couldn't hold it against Nate for having dinner with her. Still, a niggling sense of duty made him ask, "Are you free Monday? Your father wants us to go to the auction and check out the cattle.

Maybe hit up Doc Pete if he's there for some free advice."

"I've got some free advice for my dad. Don't buy any more cattle. But yeah, I'll go for a ride. It's been a while." She smiled at him and all thoughts of Doc Pete fled. "Do you want to go to the Christmas parade with me this week?"

"I have to work. Cows don't care if there's a parade going on."

"Take a day off. When was the last time you had a break?"

He didn't want to think about it. It was before Frank's first heart attack. "I can't."

She made a frustrated sound. "Why the hell not?"

"I don't want to." Being around all those happy families just made him ornery. It was the reason he had passed on going to the Corbyns' tree trimming last week. He didn't mind the grub and the free drinks, but nothing was free. You had to make small talk and eventually Clara Perkins turned her beady eyes on you and then *the Matchmaker* would make you her special project. Nate shuddered.

"It'll be fun."

"It'll be crowded. Everyone in town will be there."

"But it's pretty."

"I'll see all the decorations later. I don't have to see it when everyone else does. I know what the town looks like all done up for Christmas," Nate argued.

"You used to like to go and see it."

"I was a lot younger then," he said grimly. "So it's a no for the tree lighting and parade leading up to it, but you sold me on a quiet dinner at home tonight."

"That's something, I suppose."

They rode along in companionable silence and Nate was trying to keep himself focused on behaving himself tonight. It was just dinner. Her father still wanted her to marry Doc Pete. But what if this was his last chance? Monday, he'd be expected to hand her over to Pete and be happy for her. Couldn't he have tonight?

"I want to thank you for giving my retreat a chance," she said, giving him an adoring look that raised his blood pressure.

Clearing his throat, he said, "Well, I don't understand why people would pay to be ranch hands, but I'm not going to turn down free labor."

"It's not a job if you get to go back to your life in two weeks. It's an adventure."

Nate rolled his eyes. "It'll be an adventure all right."

Chapter Seven

J ANICE KNEW IT was ridiculous to feel nervous. She'd had dinner with Nate a thousand times. Of course, they'd never been alone. And never in his cottage. It felt a little like sneaking out her window to go drink beers under the bleachers in the summer with her friends. Only, she never wore sexy lingerie to do that. Her plan? To finish what they'd started this morning.

"Wishful thinking," she said to her reflection, but undid another button on her shirt anyway. Janice was in the mood to push her luck, though. She couldn't go on like this with him anymore. Either he wanted to be with her or he didn't. If he didn't, well there were other cowboys in the pasture. Or maybe veterinarians.

Her mind flickered on Pete, but didn't linger. It was Nate she wanted and even though her knees were shaking and she wanted to go back home until her courage returned, Janice knew it was now or never.

She could smell the steaks on the grill as she approached the cabin. Not having time to make an apple pie, she'd done the next best thing and grabbed a jar of canned peaches and made some quick whipped cream in the blender. When she had thought of other uses for the whipped cream, her throat had gotten dry and she'd almost dropped the bowl.

"It's just dinner," Janice told herself, to avoid the crushing disappointment she'd feel when it turned out to be true.

But it felt different this time.

She wanted it to be different. In all her years, this ranch, her family and Nate were the only constants in her life. The ranch could be bankrupt in a few years. Her family was changing. Her sisters were getting married and her father's health wasn't what it should be. She couldn't lose Nate, too.

He was leaning on his porch rail with a bottle of beer dangling from his fingers. Daisy lolled on the ground in front of him. The dog gave her a tail thump in greeting, but otherwise didn't move. A slight smile lingered on Nate's face as he looked her over. As promised, he had showered and his damp hair was curling at his nape.

Janice hurried over to him. "Smells good," she said. But she was talking about his aftershave, which smelled like pine and leather, rather than the steaks.

"You found a jar of peaches?" He grinned.

"It was the last one. Don't tell Mom."

"My lips are sealed," Nate said. He paused after taking them from her and then leaned in and brushed a kiss on her cheek.

Excitement fluttered through her, but he disappeared into the kitchen to set the jars on the counter.

"Steaks are just about done. Do you want wine or beer with dinner?"

"Wine," she said, thinking it would be more romantic.

He pulled out a dusty bottle. "August Wolf recommended this to me for steaks. It looks fancy, but it was only twelve bucks."

Janice preferred August's beer, but she was willing to try anything that might lower Nate's inhibitions. She set the table while he plated the steaks and baked potatoes.

"When are you going to start decorating for Christmas?" she asked.

"I'm not going to bother to put up a tree this year."

"Why not?" Plunking down into her seat, she stared at him in disbelief.

"Who the hell has time?" he said without any heat in his voice. He just sounded tired. "It's too much trouble. I have to haul it inside. Set it up. It's going to drop pine needles everywhere."

"What about an artificial tree? We can get one on Monday after the auction."

He shook his head and poured her the wine. "I'm just not feeling it this year. We're not kids anymore. Christmas is just another day."

Janice could only gape at him as he made sure Daisy had enough food and water before sitting down across the table from her.

"What's wrong?" she whispered.

"Nothing," he said, bristling. He handed her the sour cream for her potatoes, and then scooped up some butter for his.

"Next thing you're going to tell me is you're calling off the secret Santa exchange."

He snorted. "The boys would revolt if I tried that."

"You're going to let them put up a tree in the bunkhouse, right?"

"Of course."

"Just not here."

"Janice, drop it."

She didn't want to drop it. But she didn't want to ruin the night by arguing. Nate had been becoming more and more withdrawn over the years. She thought it was just the distance and because she had only seen him a few times a year, she could dismiss it as it just being Nate in a bad mood. But now that she saw him every day, she could see that the strain of taking over the physical part of running the ranch from her father had taken its toll.

"I'm looking forward to going to the auction with you," she said. She'd make sure it would be as close to a vacation day as he would let her.

Nate just ate his steak. It was delicious and she demolished half of it before she came up for air. Being out in the pastures gave her the appetite of a dragon. The wine was excellent too. She picked up the bottle and studied the label. "I'm going to have to pick some of this up."

"Sour grapes," he muttered.

"What is?"

"Wine. That's all it is."

"I don't think they let it go sour before they make it. That's vinegar. Like your attitude lately. You need a vacation."

Nate just grunted.

"I'm serious." She laid down her wineglass. "You've been working for at least six months straight without a break. No one can keep up that pace."

"I like my job," he said with a shrug. "I get to ride a horse all day and be outside. You know how that is. It's not work when you have fun."

"Are you having fun?"

"It would be a lot more fun if we were making a profit." He blew out a sigh. "I am tired, Janice. I can't deny that. But that's all it is. I need to work just as hard as everyone else to make sure we can weather the tough times. You girls were right to push to diversify the land. But in the end, the cattle are why we are here."

"I know," she said, reaching across the table to hold his hand. His palm was calloused from holding the rope and she shivered a bit, wondering what it would feel like skimming over her naked body.

His gaze turned smoky as he regarded her from across the table. "You look beautiful tonight."

Feeling a blush creeping up on her, she looked down. "I wanted to dress up a bit."

"Why?"

She stood up and walked around the table. It was now or never. Swallowing hard, she sat on his lap. "You know why."

His kiss was as sweet and sensual as she had hoped. His hand was warm on her back, holding her to him. Each brush of his lips across hers strengthened her resolve to take this as far as she could. She was terrified that he'd change his mind and leave her aching and wanting. Unbuttoning her blouse,

Janice shrugged out of it.

Nate's groan of appreciation gave her the courage to unbutton his shirt. His tongue swept against hers as he reached up and cupped her breasts. As he thumbed rough circles around her nipples, it was her turn to groan. Wiggling on his lap, she wanted more. After he slid out of his shirt, she tugged his T-shirt over his head. When she leaned down to lick at his flat, brown nipples, he stood up.

"That's it," he said. After picking her up, he carried her into the bedroom and tossed her on the bed.

Yes! Finally. Finally.

Janice flung off her shoes and pants in eager enthusiasm. Dressed only in her bra and panties, she watched Nate strip down as well. Her mouth grew dry at the sight of his rough, muscled body.

"I've wanted this for a long time," he told her and joined her. Running his hand up her leg, he kissed her belly and moved upward.

"I was yours for the taking, anytime you wanted me," she said. His mouth was hot and wet on hers.

Nate trailed his fingers over the edges of her panties. Wrapping her arms around his neck, she spread her legs wide. When he dipped his finger inside her, she cried out.

"Is that all right?" he asked, huskily. He tickled across her wet folds and she arched into his fingers.

"Yes," she breathed, reaching down to stroke his hardness. She pulled his cock out of his underwear and he hissed in a breath.

She rubbed him slowly as he fingered her. Janice indulged herself, picturing his thick length plunging inside her. She moaned as he stroked her clit while ravaging her mouth. This was what she had been dreaming of. This was what she had been waiting for.

Her breathing quickened and she jerked him off faster as his fingers drove her to madness. She didn't recognize the hungry sounds coming out of her throat. All she felt was the sweet rush of passion as it crashed in wave after wave of pleasure over her trembling body.

"That's it, darlin'. Come for me."

Shivering, she did. As she recovered from that, he stripped off her panties and then buried his face between her legs. Lapping and sucking her clit, Nate held her tight as she cried out and rubbed herself against him.

"Yes. Yes," she sobbed out, barely able to stand the joy that made her limbs shake.

He moaned and the vibrations set her off again. Janice gripped the sheets tight and stared up at the ceiling in disbelief. It was so damned good. She couldn't stop the orgasms from driving her out of her mind and she didn't want to. There wasn't any time to think about money or the ranch or anything but Nate's relentless tongue and how it was wreaking havoc on her senses. She was a quaking pile of nerves when he rose up. Kneeling above her, he put on a condom.

"Please," she whispered. She was greedy for more.

Pulling up her bra, he massaged her breasts. "I want you." His eyes were dark with need.

"Yes." Janice didn't care what he did to her as long as he

didn't stop until he came inside her. She wanted him to feel as crazy and out of control as she did.

Leaning over her, he licked her nipple and then sucked on it. Fumbling between them, Janice reached down and guided his cock inside her. Grunting, he slammed hard into her. His mouth on her throat, he made love to her with deep, long thrusts.

Janice grabbed his ass with both hands and held him deep as she clenched in pleasure around him.

"Oh, darlin'," he moaned. "I wanted to take it slow. But I can't. I can't."

"Fast now. Slow later," Janice breathed, barely able to speak.

He pumped deep and his bed creaked loud with each thrust. She wrapped her legs around his waist and held on to his shoulders as he rode her fast and hard. Each pass was delicious friction around her sensitive nerves. Janice raised her hips to meet him stroke for stroke and clamped her muscles around his cock hard when she came. She roared and pushed up at him, needing him deep. Tremors shook his powerful back as he came.

They clung to each other in a daze. Janice caressed his sweat-slick skin and enjoyed the press of his body on top of her. Entangling her legs with his, she silently urged him to spend the night inside her. But as their breathing got back to normal, Nate gently unwound himself and went to the bathroom to clean up.

"You're staying the night," he said, and it wasn't a question.

"Try and stop me," she said, smiling. Her lips were swollen and her body felt sore in the right places. When he came back to bed, she got up to wash up a bit and grabbed their wineglasses on the way back.

But Nate was already flat out, snoring.

Shrugging, Janice finished the wine in a few long swallows and then got under the covers to cuddle with him. Daisy joined them and it was crowded in a way that felt perfectly at home.

Chapter Eight

NATE AND DAISY were gone by the time she woke up. Janice stretched and smiled goofily at the ceiling. Things were starting to come together. For the first time all year, she was feeling positive about the future. After getting dressed, she hurried back to the retreat center to feed the dogs and let them out to run around in the fenced-in section that Nate and the boys put up for her. She eyed it critically as a thought popped up. With the dogs safe inside, she might be able to exercise Black Dahlia and Synergy here. Distracted, she walked the distance of the fence, mentally counting off the distance.

All King Edward's Horses Can Manage Big Fences was the mnemonic she used to remember the order of letters around a dressage arena. The letters were used as an easy way to instruct the rider where to perform different movements.

Pointing to each position where the letters AKEHCMBF would go, Janice nodded. With some extensions and fence work, she could use it as a dressage arena.

She needed to focus. Her guests weren't coming to her to learn dressage.

But would it help? Could she make dressage part of the

retreat experience? Janice's eyes misted up. It would be perfect, just like she had said to Nate. Dressage was a discipline that required concentration, and like meditation, it could really help center the rider and teach her about trusting and handling a horse.

She took in a shaky breath. Could she teach the basics? Janice snorted. More than that. Her father would shit, though. The only thing he hated more than dressage was the Texas A&M Aggies. Nodding in satisfaction, she thought it would serve him right for leveling her old ring. She would have to check her lease to see if he had to approve any modifications to the retreat center. The bank wouldn't be too thrilled that she was spending more money, but that's why she had the loan. Like she'd told Nate, they had to diversify to make some money.

The more she thought about it, the more it seemed like a good idea. Maybe building the dressage arena could be a team-building exercise that Rita's group could help her with. It would keep them out of Nate's hair for most of the week and they could bond with their horses.

Janice threw the balls and Frisbees for the dogs, laughing as they tumbled over themselves to chase them. Leaving the dogs to enjoy the crisp morning air, Janice took a quick shower. Afterward, she did some last-minute cleaning in anticipation of her guests who were coming today and then headed over to the barn with all the dogs in tow.

Kelly and Alissa were cleaning up and Janice saw that Synergy and Black Dahlia had already been taken care of. Alissa squealed at the sight of her six pups and sank down to her knees to be swarmed by them.

"Where were you this morning?" Kelly asked with a raise of her eyebrow. She had to stand flat against the wall to avoid being trampled by the eager dogs. Synergy kicked the stall in protest.

"I had some things to do before Rita and her group arrive." Janice hoped her sister didn't notice the beard burns on her neck that Nate had left last night. It wasn't chilly enough to wear a sweater, but her high-collared shirt should cover most of the marks. Her breasts throbbed at the memory of having his rough cheeks between her legs.

"How many are coming for the retreat?" Kelly asked, soothing Synergy before Janice had a chance to comfort her horse. She settled for combing through Black Dahlia's mane.

"Six. Two to a bedroom. Rita is staying at her place and I'll be…" Oh shit. "I'll be back in my old room at the ranch house." With her mother and father. Where sneaking out would put her back in the high school frame of mind again. She sure as hell wasn't ready to tell her father she was sleeping with his foreman. That was something they should ease into—maybe get through the holidays first so Christmas wasn't an awkward rage-fueled affair, like it had been after Kelly had left.

"I knew you could do it." Kelly gave her a quick hug. "Let me know if your group wants a portrait. I'll cut them a deal."

"Actually yeah, put me down for a group portrait. If they want individual ones, I'll send them to you."

"My treat," Kelly said.

Janice was going to protest, but Kelly cut her off. "It's part of the Sullivan package deal."

"Well, if you're sure."

"I am and it will be another way to get exposure for my business. You want me to talk to Trent about giving them some rudimentary bull-riding lessons?"

"They're not going to be able to ride a bull in two weeks," Janice said, exasperated.

"No, but the mechanical bull is perfectly safe."

"That might be a fun way to spend one of the weekend nights. I'll run it by Rita. We don't have a lot of structure, but I'm getting them up early tomorrow to help take care of the horses and the first calf heifers."

"Are you sure they're paying you to shovel sh—" Kelly cut herself off after realizing Alissa was paying close attention to their conversation. "Cow manure?"

"It's all part of the confidence-building exercises."

"Uh-huh," Kelly said. "Sounds a bit Tom Sawyerish, if you ask me. But we could use the extra hands now that…" She trailed off again, this time in sadness rather than censoring herself.

"Yeah, Nate told me he had to let some of the ranch hands go."

"I thought we were winning," Kelly whispered, stepping away from Alissa so her daughter wouldn't hear the anguish in her voice. They were safe, though. Trent had purchased the land outright from her father and their new house was going to be a place where Kelly would never have to worry about being kicked out or having the land sold because of bankruptcy. Even if Kelly's portrait studio and Trent's riding school went bust, they had a nice nest egg from Trent's pro bull riding winnings.

The rest of them, however, weren't so lucky. Her father kept joking that Emily and Janice should find some rich husbands, too. It started to become less and less funny as the winter months approached and the bills started to pile up again.

"We're not giving up," Janice said. "It's a roller-coaster ride though. All these ups and downs. Rita's group is just what we need to keep our heads above water."

Ever since they had come to an agreement, Janice and Rita spoke a few times each day. The six women coming to the retreat had been in therapy together for about a year, so they all knew each other. Rita couldn't tell her any details, of course, but based on the activities she requested to have Janice line up, Janice figured that they could use a place to do physical work and go to bed exhausted, but with a feeling of accomplishment.

And if she could teach a few how to ride and a few more how to camp, Janice would consider the first week a success. Rita was doing the heavy stuff—the mental therapy. Janice was assisting with the physical therapy. Which reminded her…

"Does your friend Zoraya still make house calls? Those women are going to need a massage after their first day."

"Yeah. If you want, I'll call her. Her rates are reasonable and she'll even bring her own table."

"Perfect." Janice picked up Alissa and spun her around

before putting her back on the ground as the little girl giggled. "I've got to go and do some retreat stuff. I'll see you later."

"Don't worry about anything. Emily and I are covering the chores and helping Mom."

Janice felt a pang of guilt, but Kelly was being sincere. "You sure you don't have any sittings scheduled?"

"Not until Trent's class comes in after school. A few mamas want to have their sons on a bucking bull as their Christmas card."

"Well, who wouldn't?" Janice smiled. When she and her sisters barrel raced in the rodeo, her mother took tons of pictures. Sarah would have loved to have some professional photos to frame and hang up on the wall.

"Can we have us bull riding on our card?" Alissa asked.

"No," Janice and Kelly said in unison. Trent's manager and father, Billy King, would lose his shit if Trent was dumb enough to get on a bull again. Trent walked with a limp and used a cane after his last ride with Corazon del Diablo. Now, the closest thing he got to that bull was impregnating some of her father's breeding stock with the stud's semen in hopes of getting a winning bull.

Those were more things that would benefit the ranch in the long run. Janice just had to help get them through until the roller coaster started climbing upward again.

"I'll see you guys later." Feeling like a slacker, Janice rounded up the pups with a whistle and hand gestures and took them inside.

"There are my furry grandbabies," Sarah said as they all

entered the house. "Can you set them up out back with some water?"

Since out back was also fenced in and had plenty of shade, Janice let the dogs roam around. She hoped the squirrels were forewarned enough that they escaped, but judging from the barking and happy dogs thundering around the area, something was being pursued.

"What time are your guests arriving?" her mother asked.

"Three. I wanted to drop the dogs off so they're out of the way while I move back in for the next two weeks. Are you sure that's okay? I know they can be a handful."

"They're fine." Sarah waved her hand. "If you're on your way back to the retreat center, take this tray of lasagna I made and the platter of cookies. You should have dinner with them tonight to make them feel welcome."

"Mom, you didn't have to do that." Tears pricked at the corner of Janice's eyes. She couldn't help getting all choked up from the help her family was giving her. She should have thought of dinner, but everything had been such a whirlwind since she booked Rita's retreat. She had lists upon lists, but had still managed to miss that one important thing. Her guests needed to feel welcome. They needed to feel safe and secure at the ranch and Janice couldn't think of anything better than her mother's homemade lasagna.

"I was making a few trays for the chuck wagon. What's one more?"

"A lot." Janice hugged her mother.

The phone rang in the kitchen. They had a landline with an ancient receiver and cradle mounted on the wall. Janice was closer, so she picked it up. "Sullivan Ranch," she said.

"Janice, unlock the front gate for the ambulance." Her father's breathing was ragged and he sounded like he was in a wind tunnel. "It's on the way."

Her knees wobbled and fear seared an icy trail down her throat. "Dad, what's wrong? Are you having another heart attack?"

Her mother gripped her arm, her eyes reflecting the same panic.

"No, I'm fine. It's Nate."

"Nate?" she screeched. Her stomach churned and she gripped the receiver tightly. "What happened?"

"Rattlesnake bit his horse and it shied and took off. Nate got thrown."

"Oh my God, is he all right?" Janice put her hand over the mouthpiece of the phone. "Nate got thrown," she told her mother.

Sarah tugged off her apron and rolled it into a ball.

"He's banged up a bit," her father said. He sounded shaken and winded.

"Are you all right?"

Sarah looked up from where she was rooting around in her purse.

"I'm fine," he snapped. "I was in the truck."

Thank goodness for small favors. Janice nodded at her mother. Sarah sighed in relief. "Did Nate hit his head?"

"He hit everything. I think he broke his shoulder."

"Let me talk to him."

"He's out cold."

"Here's Mom." Janice gave her the phone. "I'm going to go out and wait for the ambulance."

Rushing outside, she had a moment to wonder what they had done about his horse. Hopefully, one of the ranch hands roped it and put a compression wrap around the wound to slow the venom. Usually a horse was too large to get a fatal dose. But if the snake bit it on the nose, there was a chance of swelling that could block the horse from breathing. They didn't have any antitoxin on hand, so she called Dr. Pete.

He answered just as she was starting up the Gator to drive to the ranch gates.

"Janice, what a lovely surprise. Your retreat is starting today, isn't it?"

"Yes," she said, feeling out of breath and weak. She had forgotten that the women were going to start arriving in the next three hours. Slamming her foot down on the accelerator, Janice drove the Gator as fast as she dared one-handed. "Unfortunately, I'm not calling because of good news. Nate's horse got bitten by a snake out in the pastures. Nate got thrown and an ambulance is on the way."

"I'm sorry to hear that. I can be there in about a half hour."

"Thanks, Pete. I don't have much information."

"Not a problem. Take care of Nate and I'll see to the horse."

"Thank you," she said, sighing.

When she got to the gates, it was eerily quiet. Unlocking them, she stepped back as they swung open wide. Straining her ears, she heard a faint siren in the distance. Looking out toward the pastures, she could just about make out her father's truck, kicking up large clouds of dust as he drove back to the ranch.

"Please be all right," she whispered, willing them to go faster.

The ambulance beat her father by about five minutes and drove to meet him halfway down the road. Hopping back on the Gator, Janice followed at maximum speed...which wasn't very fast.

They were loading Nate into the ambulance when she finally caught up.

"Dad," she said, stopping dead in her tracks. The paramedics were fussing over him, too. "He has a bad heart," she said to them.

"I told them that," Frank snapped, but it had less bite to it than usual.

"We'd like for you to come to the hospital as well, Mr. Sullivan."

"I'm fine. I didn't fall off my horse. I didn't get bitten."

"Dad, maybe you should go with them. I'll come with you."

"I thought you had your boohoo group coming in today."

"I do, but you two are more important." Janice realized she didn't have her purse on her or any of her father's medical records. "Let me drive you back to the house and we can go to Jameson together."

"You can drive me back, but your mother can take me." He sagged against the trunk. "I'm not feeling so well."

That was a bad sign. Frank Sullivan never admitted to weakness.

"Why don't you go and ride in the ambulance? Mom and I will meet you at the hospital."

"No, we're just going to wait around for hours. No sense in you missing your people." He moved gingerly around the truck to get in the passenger side. As the paramedics helped him, Janice climbed into the ambulance where another paramedic was working on Nate.

Nate was conscious and looking confused. "What happened?"

"You tell me," the paramedic said.

"Where am I?"

"Nate, you got thrown from your horse." Janice reached for his hand and squeezed it.

"Janice." He tried for a smile, but winced. "What are you doing here?"

"How is he?" she asked the paramedic.

"He took a hard knock. Definitely a concussion and I'm worried about that shoulder."

"Hurts," Nate said.

"Don't close your eyes," the paramedic said and then turned to her. "Are you coming to the hospital with us? Because we've got to get moving."

Janice leaned forward and kissed Nate on the cheek. "Behave," she said. "I need to help my dad."

"Is Frank all right?"

"He's fine. Be a good patient."

Nate snorted, then winced.

Janice looked back as she jumped down from the ambulance. She was second-guessing herself. She wanted to go with Nate, but she was worried about her father. In the end, her dithering caused the decision to be made for her as the ambulance crew got back inside and sped away.

"Can't afford another hospital bill," her father mumbled.

"Can't afford not to have one," she said lightly, but knew he was right. They both were.

Leaving the Gator, Janice sent a text to Emily to come pick it up. She drove carefully back to the ranch house and met her mother at the door.

"We need to take him to Jameson for some tests."

"I said I'm fine." Frank slid out of the truck and stood shakily on his feet.

"The paramedic wanted you to get looked at."

"You need to see about that horse." Frank walked gingerly on his own to the porch steps. "I'll be all right. I just need to sit a spell. Sarah, can you get me a cold drink?"

"Fine," Janice said. "I'm going to the hospital, then."

But as the words left her mouth, Doc Pete pulled up.

"I need you to go with him out to Bushwacker and take a look at the horse." Her father named his pastures after famous PBR bulls. "I'm glad to see you, Pete. But I wished she hadn't called you."

"We don't have any antitoxins," Janice said.

"Maybe we should." Her father arched her a look.

Janice glared back at him. Now was not the time for him to start in on her about her occupation.

"It's all right. I'm here now. We'll figure the rest out later." Pete laid a comforting hand on her shoulder and she sagged in defeat. If she didn't go with Pete, chances were, her father would. If he wasn't going to the hospital, he needed to stay here under her mother's watchful eyes. And Nate was in good hands at Jameson. She could go visit him once her guests were settled.

Janice nodded. "I suppose I should keep more supplies stocked for emergencies."

Her father grinned wide and waved as she got into Pete's truck. Janice wasn't convinced he hadn't hit his head as well.

Chapter Nine

B RUSSELS SPROUTS.
Saddle sores.

Nate was still groggy from the anesthetic they gave him before putting his dislocated shoulder back into position. Yeah, that was fun. Now, he was trying to list all the things he liked better than being in a hospital. And to put the cherry on this shit sundae, he couldn't even take a nap. If it wasn't all the movement in and around his room, it was his mind thinking of something else that needed to get done. Every time he tried to drift off, something startled him awake.

He was waiting for his CAT scan appointment and he was sure that he was just about to fall asleep when they woke him up to take him down there. Nate tried to use his phone, but he couldn't seem to get his eyes to focus. Maybe this was a weird kind of karma. It had been a nap that got him into this mess in the first place.

Damn it. He knew better than to be distracted in the saddle. He hoped his horse was all right. If Nate hadn't been snoozing in the saddle, he might have seen or heard the rattlesnake and guided Jonas away from it. But Jonas stuck his big nose into the snake's personal space and got bit. Nate might have stayed on if he had a better grip on the saddle horn, but when Jonas jumped and tore off, Nate had taken a header.

He supposed he should feel lucky that Jonas dragged him away from the snake before Nate kicked out of the stirrups. But man, he had done a number on his shoulder. He didn't remember hitting his head. Didn't remember much of anything until Janice kissed him in the ambulance. Nate frowned, and then winced as the pain hit him hard. Where was she?

Using his phone when one arm was in a sling made his shoulder scream in pain. He dialed her number, slowly, painstakingly, and his head was throbbing by the time the call connected. It rang forever and then went to her voice mail.

"Hey, can you bring me a beer and a pulled pork sandwich from The Hut? Call me. I feel like shit."

Nate huffed. That really wasn't what he had wanted to say. After all, last night had been so fantastic that he almost stayed in bed with her for the entire day. Of course, someone would have come looking for him—probably her father—and he didn't want to have to deal with that baggage so early in the morning. Or ever, really.

It wasn't that she had worn him out. He'd never complain about that. But he had been going nonstop for most of the year. Having the best sex of his life must have signaled his body that it was done working overtime. And while it was taking it easy in the warm sun, Nate paid the price for sleeping on the job. He just hoped he wouldn't have to pay the price for sleeping with the boss's daughter.

He tried calling the ranch. And after the third time, Nate managed to punch in the right numbers.

"Sullivan Ranch," a bright and cheery voice said.

"Janice?" he croaked.

"No, this is Emily."

"Emily, it's Nate."

"Nate!"

Her squeal made him wince and pull the phone away from his ear.

"How are you?"

"I'm all right. Where's Janice?"

"She's still with Doc Pete."

What the hell? "I thought she was heading up here with Frank?"

Emily sighed. "Yeah, that stubborn old coot is refusing to go."

"I heard that," Frank yelled out in the background. "Tell Nate not to worry about anything. We've got it covered."

"I'm sure you can hear him," Emily said. "Esteban is going to step up while you're gone."

"I'm not gone," Nate grumbled. "I just have to stay overnight."

Why is Janice with Doc Pete?

"They're looking at Jonas. It doesn't look good."

"Damn it, Emily. Don't tell the man that," Frank snapped.

It took Nate a minute to realize that he had asked the

question aloud. He had better be more careful. It took another second or two before he realized what Emily had said. "Jonas? Damn. Was it the venom?" He couldn't believe a rattlesnake could take down a big horse like that.

"No. It was a reaction to the bite. He was having trouble breathing and then his nostrils closed up. I guess they have him on some kind of horse Benadryl or something. I'm going out there in a few minutes because Janice's retreat group is going to arrive very soon."

Right. That was today. Hell, his head hurt so bad, he was having trouble concentrating or remembering things. "Tell her to call me," he said.

"I will. But you get some rest and let the doctors and nurses take care of you. Give us a call when you're allowed to come home and one of us will come and get you."

"Thanks," he said gruffly and hung up the phone before Emily could hear the emotion in his voice. The Three Sisters Ranch was his home. He couldn't just lie in bed while the bill collectors came knocking on the doors.

Nate squinted around the room, looking for his clothes. All he saw were faded holiday decorations and a tree that Charlie Brown would be embarrassed to own on the window ledge in the corner. He tried to get up, but sitting made him dizzy and he slumped back into bed. He supposed one day of rest wouldn't hurt. It seemed like such a waste that he'd have to be alone though.

Especially when Janice had spent her day with Doc Pete.

Nate tried to take advantage of being prone and groggy to catch up on some much-needed sleep, but he still couldn't get his mind to shut down. The antiseptic smell bothered him and the strange noises kept him on edge.

What if Esteban does a better job than me?
What if they realize that they don't need me anymore?
What if Janice really does marry Doc Pete?
How am I supposed to act seeing them together?

Groaning, Nate shifted on his good side and stared at the wall. This wasn't him. It must be the stupid medication they gave him. Closing his eyes, he tried to shut it all out. But the unfamiliar atmosphere kept him on edge and allowed the monkeys in his brain out of their cages for the first time in twenty years.

He was seven years old again, sitting on a box in a back room somewhere, watching an illegal poker game. They were in Odessa, maybe or El Paso. The places they went all blurred together. His father was losing money he didn't have, and Nate was worried he was going to take it out on him later. Nate remembered wondering if he could steal a bottle of whiskey to distract his old man with later.

"I don't want to think about this," Nate said aloud.

But it didn't stop the memory. He almost called for the nurse. But what if she gave him something that knocked him out? Then he'd be helpless against the rush of feelings coming at him.

"It's bullshit," he muttered. "All bullshit."

He had tried not to fidget or distract any of the players. Why the old man hadn't left him in the car, he didn't know.

Yes, he did.

"Are you looking forward to Christmas, kid?" one of the poker players asked during the shuffle.

Christmas was just another day, but Nate knew enough not to say that. That would call attention to himself and earn him a beating.

"Yes, sir," he had said, hoping that was the end of it when his father had glared at him.

"What do you want Santa to bring you?"

"A puppy," he had blurted out. Stupid. They didn't even have a house. Heck, they could barely feed themselves. Getting a puppy was about as real as Santa coming down a chimney they didn't even have.

"Every kid should have a dog," another player had said.

The other players had nodded, while his father had just grunted.

"It was a long time ago," Nate said aloud.

The game hadn't been going well for his father, but he had built up a substantial stack of chips. Still, it hadn't been enough when it was down to him and the leader.

"I'm all in," the leader had said, pushing in several stacks of chips—a lot more than what his father had in front of him.

"I know you're bluffing."

But his father's pile would only earn him double what he put in and Nate had seen the glimmer of greed in his father's eyes.

"How much you got there?" he had asked the leader.

"Twenty-five thousand dollars."

Nate's father had trickled his chips through his fingers. "I've got five."

"Five will get you ten." The leader had grinned.

"I want to bet the full twenty-five."

The leader had chortled. "Too bad you don't have that."

His father had jerked his thumb at him. "The boy's worth the difference."

"Jesus," one of the other players, who had mucked his hand a few bets ago, had said.

Another player, who had busted an hour ago, turned around from the makeshift bar and said, "Now, we got a card game."

The leader had looked Nate over critically. "Why not? It's Christmas after all."

"Are you ready for your CAT scan, Mr. Pierson."

"Hell, yeah," Nate said, relieved to be interrupted.

AFTER THE CAT scan, Nate was hoping they would let him go home. But it was another waiting game. At least he wasn't assaulted by memories this time. He glared up at the ceiling and willed himself to fall asleep. And he did, in fits and starts. His head hurt like a bitch.

The doctor came in a few hours later. "You're cleared to go home."

"Finally." Nate tried to drape his legs over the bed, but couldn't quite get them to move.

The doctor held up a hand. "Hold on there. I want you to stay the night, just in case. You can go home first thing in the morning. I wanted to talk to you about some other symptoms we noticed."

Nate suppressed a groan. That was the trouble with doctors. They always found something wrong with you. "Is it my heart?" He wondered if he was going down the same road Frank was traveling.

"No, your EKG matches the baseline that you took at your last physical. But I'm not too happy about your blood pressure."

"I feel fine," Nate croaked.

"I was looking at your answers on your intake form and I think there's a bigger problem going on, aside from your concussion."

Nate should have prettied up what he had put on the forms, but his head had hurt too much to think up good lies. He knew he was burning the candle at both ends and it was starting to catch up to him. There wasn't a hell of a lot he could do about it until they could hire more men, Frank got better, or they brought the ranch back into the black. There was no sense wishing things were different.

"I've got everything under control," he said.

"What were you doing before your horse got bit?"

He gave a long sigh. Nate just wanted to go home. Or have the doctor leave him alone. But the best way to do that was answer his questions. "We had just finished bringing the cattle into Bushwacker pasture. I was supervising the feeding and checking the cattle."

"Have you been getting enough sleep?"

"I had a late night, last night." Nate refused to elaborate.

It was none of the doc's business what had happened.

"Does that happen a lot?"

Nate couldn't resist a bark of laughter, but immediately regretted it when pain lanced through his skull.

"Not as much as I'd like," he said, accepting the Tylenol and the water that the doctor handed him from the side table.

"You mentioned having trouble sleeping."

"I've got a lot on my mind."

"And that things seem to bother you more than they should. Have you noticed a difference in your appetite?"

Shrugging, Nate crossed his arms over his chest. "I'm all right. I eat when I'm hungry or when I get back from the barn."

"Have you been more stressed at work lately?"

"You could say that."

"Care to elaborate?"

Nate wondered if the doctor was a headshrinker, because Nate didn't need to get in touch with his feelings. That was Janice and her retreat's area. "My boss, Frank Sullivan, has been in and out of the hospital and I've been picking up the slack for the last year. There's been a lot of long, hard hours, but that's what ranching is."

"I hear the ranch is in trouble."

Nate bristled. "Well, don't believe everything you hear."

"I only mention it because I think you're emotionally exhausted."

"What the hell does that mean?"

"I think you're burned out."

"Better to burn out, than fade away," Nate quipped.

"Not really," the doctor said dryly. "Look, you need to give your body what it wants."

An image of Janice naked, underneath him, floated through Nate's mind. "I'll see what I can do."

"Sleep at least eight hours a night."

Nate snorted. "Doc, I'm up at four a.m. and I don't get home until six. You can't expect me to go to bed at nine. I'm not a kid."

"Then you're going to have to play catch-up on the weekends."

"I don't have a Monday through Friday job."

"You need to take a few days off or work shorter hours."

Nate shook his head, but immediately regretted it. "I can't do that."

"If you want your shoulder to heal, you have to keep it in a sling, ice it down, and let it rest. While you're resting it, you need to concentrate on keeping your stress levels down."

"I don't sit still well when there's things to be done."

"Then, it's time to delegate." The doctor ticked off on his fingers. "Sleep, relaxation, eat three healthy meals a day, and get a better work-life balance."

"Yeah, yeah." Nate tried to be pleasant, but it was wearing thin.

"Look, your body is going to revolt. First, it'll be nodding off in the saddle."

Nate clenched his jaw.

"Then, your irritability, brain fog and other symptoms will get worse. Nip it in the bud while you can. And if you can't, we can talk about some medication that can help you."

No more medication. It made him dwell on the past. And the past couldn't be changed. "I'm all right, Doc. I just need some sleep and what you said, life-balance shit."

The doctor gave a resigned sigh. "All right." He put out his hand to shake. "I hope I won't see you back here anytime soon. I'll arrange for your discharge paperwork so they're ready for you first thing in the morning."

"I'd appreciate that," Nate said.

"Get some rest."

"I'll try." But Nate was already thinking about the work he would need to catch up on when he got back to the ranch tomorrow.

Chapter Ten

JANICE WAS STILL trying to memorize the women's names. She had written them down in her book of lists with a description to help her remember something unique about them. But she was too distracted about Jonas and Nate.

She hoped Nate was doing better than Jonas. She didn't want to call Nate's hospital room in case he was sleeping, but he sounded so grumpy on her voice mail, she didn't want to deal with his temper if she didn't call.

Slipping the phone in her pocket, she decided to call him later that evening. Rita helped Janice settle the women into their rooms. A few of them turned their noses up at the simple accommodations, but there wasn't much Janice could do to help them out.

Rita had a session with them after they settled in and Janice took that time to make sure her supplies for building the dressage ring had come in. That was the group's first project after they got the lay of the land tomorrow morning, along with an early breakfast with the ranch hands. Janice was hoping that at the end of the day tomorrow, they'd go to bed tired, but with a feeling of accomplishment. Then every day, they could build on that.

Over dinner that night, the women bonded over her mother's lasagna and while they were cleaning up, Janice nudged Rita. "Can I talk to you a moment?"

"Sure."

"Monday, Nate and I are going to the cattle auction." Janice was going to convince him to let her drive so he could take it easy. She wasn't looking forward to that argument.

"What a great idea! I think by then, they're going to want a bit of a break."

"Oh." Janice hadn't considered taking them. She was going to ask if it was all right if Emily could take over their riding lessons for the day.

"And then Friday, we'll have the Christmas parade in the morning and then the tree lighting at night. This is going to be a great week." Rita's smile faltered. "What's wrong?"

"Don't mind me. I'm just worried about Nate and his horse Jonas." Janice had already explained what had happened to everyone.

"They'll be fine. From what you told me, they're tough. And Jonas couldn't be in any better hands than with Peter."

Janice blinked. She hadn't ever heard anyone call Doc Pete, Peter before. "That's for sure," she said. "Do you think these guys are going to regret coming here when we wake them up at four in the morning?"

Rita laughed. "They signed up for this."

"I hope I don't disappoint them," Janice said, feeling a flush of embarrassment creep up her cheeks.

"Just show them the ranch life that you grew up with and your enthusiasm will make this the best two-week retreat of their lives."

Janice nodded. "I hope so."

By the time they wrapped up for the night, visiting hours at the hospital were over. Janice was feeling restless. Back at the ranch house, her parents were settling down for an evening of snoozing in front of the television. Three of her dogs were on the couch with her mother. Bowser was in her father's lap and the other two were by his reclining chair. They looked up and thumped their tails at her, but otherwise, they didn't get up to greet her.

Traitors.

"How did your first day go?" her mother asked, looking up from her knitting.

"Good. I think it's going to be a mutually beneficial relationship."

Her father snorted. "I think you hustled those women out of their money."

"Frank," her mother said warningly.

"Dad, I'm giving them an experience they've never had and it's going to help build their confidence."

"You're using them as unpaid labor."

"I'm giving them a chance to be part of a group. Unlike being a drone in a major corporation, they can see how the work they do on this ranch immediately benefits someone or something. That's very powerful."

"You should have been a politician instead of a vet tech," he said.

"Well since I am a vet tech, I talked with Doc Pete about this and we're both in agreement that you're moving the cattle too often. They're going to get sick if you keep up the pace."

"You let me handle that part."

"Don't make me go over your head to Emily," Janice said.

"Over my head? I still run this ranch," her father said, heatedly.

"You wanted a large-animal vet on the ranch? Well, Pete's a large-animal vet and he agrees with me. You're running your ranch hands and your cattle too hard."

"They need the exercise and we need to make sure the pastures are sustainable."

"It's too late for that this year. We're supplementing with hay and feed. Don't rotate them so much."

Frank waved his hand in disgust at her. "I'm watching my programs. Leave me be."

Janice wanted to snap back at him, but that would only prolong the argument. She would have this discussion with Emily and Emily could handle their father. She turned back to her mother. "Do we still have any old Christmas stuff in the attic or has Emily taken it all?"

"I don't know," Sarah said. "She was decorating Donovan's hunting lodge the other day, so who knows what's left."

"When are we putting our tree up?" she asked.

"After the Christmas Ball. Have you gotten a dress yet?"

The annual Christmas Ball was going to be held at Jameson House this year. They were raising funds for the Last Stand Rodeo's scholarship funds and to maintain the rodeo grounds that could use a good coat of paint.

"Not yet. Kelly and Emily and I are going to go looking next weekend." Janice would have rather gotten something online, but her sisters had browbeat her until she'd agreed to go to the mall with them. She'd rather be bitten by a rattlesnake than brave the malls at Christmastime.

"I'm going to wear my red pants suit," Sarah said.

"Didn't you wear that last year?" Janice crinkled her nose.

"So what? No one is going to care."

"You should come with us."

"Not on your life," Sarah said. "If I wanted to get stampeded, I'd go out into the pasture in my red pants suit."

Janice grinned and headed up to the attic. It bothered her that Nate hadn't felt like decorating for Christmas. She was going to see what she could do to give his cottage a little bit of holiday spirit.

Pulling on the string that clicked on the light, she squinted in the semidarkness of the attic. Janice saw a few holiday boxes that Emily hadn't gotten her hands on yet and pulled them over to the nursery rocker that her mom had used when they had been babies. It was soft and comfortable. Curling her legs underneath her, she lifted a box into her lap and went through the contents.

She found a snow globe that had lost some water, but inside, Santa and Mrs. Claus were still packing up the sleigh. She remembered her dad buying it for her mom one year as a surprise. Christmas was the one time of year her father actually seemed to enjoy, and he tried not to let his temper run out of control. Any other month, it was open season, though.

He had kicked Kelly out when she was pregnant in May.

He had hassled Emily for being a vegetarian so much, she ran off to Africa the first chance she got.

And Janice had accepted the first job that she had been offered right out of college. Kentucky had been the farthest she had gone.

She had felt bad about leaving Nate. But the family always came back for the holidays. Except during that awful time when Kelly and her father hadn't been speaking. Alissa's first Christmas still brought tears to her eyes. Angry and sad ones. Janice rocked faster on the chair to push aside those unhappy memories. But they lingered, like the faint dust motes around the light bulb.

If Nate hadn't been there, it would have been a disaster. He had snuck Emily and her out of the house early in the morning so they could watch Alissa's look at the tree all lit up for the first time via FaceTime. After the phone call, he made them breakfast while they tried to make it look like they hadn't been crying. They decorated his living room as an excuse, just in case anyone asked where they had been.

Nate had taken it with good grace, but Janice knew he wouldn't have put up the garland or the small tree by himself.

She had asked him why and he had told her that he hated the expectation of Christmas that people who were utter shits the rest of the year would behave themselves in hopes that Santa wouldn't put them on the naughty list. And then, he had said, there were the ones that got worse, because they knew Christmas was just a scam.

Janice hated when he got like that. His father had done a number on him and she was glad she'd never got to meet him. She'd probably run him over with the Gator. Twice.

But the parts of Christmas that were special were in those quiet moments. Janice and Nate would break out the Monopoly game and play cutthroat for hours while drinking hot apple cider or hard cider depending on what time of day it was. Her mother would be singing carols in the kitchen and Dad would be watching football. Their busy life stopped for one day.

Sure, the animals still got fed and taken care of, but at a slower pace.

Sometimes Janice wished every day was Christmas. But she supposed if it was, it wouldn't be special anymore. Picking out a bunch of things she thought Nate would like, she carefully took them with her. Soon it would be time to put up their tree and she was starting to get that giddy feeling in her stomach again. This Christmas was going to be the best one yet.

Chapter Eleven

WHEN FOUR A.M. rolled around the next morning, Janice was amused to see six groggy women stumble out of their rooms. They no longer seemed so keen on the idea of being on a working ranch.

"I'm used to going to bed at this hour," Regina said, groaning and stretching. She ran a bar in San Antonio. She had short purple hair that stood up straight on end as she ran her fingers through it and stifled a yawn with her other hand.

"Not me," Suze said, gathering her chestnut hair back into a tight ponytail. "It's a relief not to get up and bake."

"Please tell me there's coffee?" Tracie said, walking out wearing baggy sweats. Her long black curls were all over the place and she just blew them out of her face as she looked around for the coffeepot. She was a kindergarten teacher with a vocabulary that could make the most seasoned ranch hand blush.

"We're going to head over to the ranch house for breakfast. Don't worry, there's plenty of coffee," Janice said, feeling a little unsure about needling them to get a move on.

"Do I have time for a morning jog before we get started today?" Gayle said, raising her hand. She was already show-cred and dressed in running shorts and sneakers.

Janice wasn't sure how to even answer that. "Not before breakfast. Maybe later though? We've got a pretty tight schedule this morning."

"I just want to make sure I get some exercise in."

Janice remembered that Gayle worked as a telemarketer, even though she hated the job. "Don't worry. You'll get plenty of exercise today."

"Just let me get my makeup on," Heidi said. Heidi had fiery-red hair and a complexion that looked like it never saw the sun. Janice would have told her not to worry about the makeup, but she thought she might need the SPF protection from her foundation. She was a chemist and worked in a lab all day.

Melanie was halfway out the door. "I'll meet you guys over there."

"Wait for the group," Rita said. "We're all in this together, remember?"

Melanie blew out an exasperated sigh and folded her arms over her chest. Melanie had energy pouring out of her in waves and Janice got jittery just standing next to her. Leaning against the wall, Melanie glared at Heidi until she finished putting on her lipstick.

Thankfully, Janice managed to get everyone to the bunkhouse for breakfast before the ranch hands rode out and by the time bacon, scrambled eggs and toast were consumed, everyone was marginally more awake and ready to start the day.

"Are we riding out today?" Tracie asked. Janice wanted

to check her notes, but she was pretty sure Tracie was one of the women who had never been on a horse before.

"No. Today we're going to work around the ranch a bit. We're going to feed the animals and I'm going to introduce you to our pregnant cows. After lunch, we're going to saddle up and take a tour of the ranch." Janice had cleared it with Donovan. He was going to come with them in case the feral hogs decided to make an appearance. She was hoping, though, that they could get by without that little bit of drama.

While they worked their way around the ranch, feeding and watering the animals, Janice gave them a history of the ranch. And of the town of Last Stand.

"When we go to the Christmas parade next week, be sure to check out the Last Stand Saloon. There are bullet holes in the limestone walls from the battle where the townsfolk held off troops from Santa Anna's army. Later on Friday night at the tree lighting, you'll see the statue of Asa Fuhrmann, who was wounded getting ammo while the original settlers were making their last stand. He later died from his wounds. And the town was named Last Stand."

Just as she was finishing her story, she saw her parents' car pass the road and caught a brief glimpse of Nate as they drove by to drop him off at his cabin. She waved, but she wasn't sure if he saw her or not.

While everyone was in the kitchen helping her mother with lunch for the chuck wagon, Janice slipped out the back and headed over to Nate's with a pot of chicken soup and a basket of snowflake rolls.

Daisy barked happily at her, but Nate scowled when he opened the door. "Quiet, Daisy. I've got a bitch of a headache."

"Hello to you, too," Janice said, kissing him on the cheek as she pushed by him into the house. "Are you hungry?"

"No," Nate grumbled. "My stomach is up in arms from the meds they gave me."

"A bowl of chicken noodle soup will make you feel better."

"Put it on the stove. I'll have it for dinner." He flipped up the towel covering the basket and snagged a dinner roll.

"How's your shoulder?" she asked as she put everything in the kitchen.

"Fine," he said, glaring at the sling.

"Are you going to take it easy today?"

"Got no choice, but I'll be back at work tomorrow."

"Don't push yourself."

"Let it be. I don't have it in me to argue with you today. Although, I distinctly remember saying I didn't want any decorations up." He jerked his chin at the small four-foot artificial tree, which she had put up in the corner of his living room.

"We wouldn't be arguing, if you'd just agree with me."

He cracked a grin. "I suppose life would be simpler if I did that."

"Do you really hate it?" She went over to the tree and straightened some of the tinsel.

"No." He sighed. "It was a nice surprise."

She had left the lights twinkling on all night, but she saw

he had shut them off. "It needs some more ornaments. Don't you have a box of them somewhere?"

"Somewhere," he said. He went into his bedroom and she followed him, trying not to seem too eager.

She sat on his bed and tried her best to look alluring, but he didn't so much as glance her way. Rummaging around in his bureau drawer, he pulled out a ceramic ornament. It was a beagle with a Christmas bow. She had given it to him last year.

"We'll put this one up for Daisy," he said.

"Daisy." She nodded and lay back on the bed.

"Now that's a tempting sight," he drawled.

"Come lie down with me. I know your shoulder is hurting, but I just want to be here with you in the peace and quiet."

Nate hesitated and she could see that he was having an argument with himself.

"Something wrong?"

"You should go back to your retreat before they notice you're gone."

"Are you trying to get rid of me?" Janice hoped that came out lighthearted and not all quivering and vulnerable.

"Of course not. I just don't want to be a nuisance."

"You're not a nuisance. I was really worried about you." She jumped up and hugged him, making sure not to jostle his arm.

"I'm fine. The doctor slammed my shoulder back into the socket. It was dislocated, not broken. It's just sore and my head is throbbing. I'm not good company."

She leaned up on her tiptoes and brushed a kiss across his lips. "So what else is new?"

The kiss brought a smile out of him. "How long have you got?" He reached down and cupped her ass.

"Not that long, unfortunately. Maybe later."

He moved his hand up to her back and rubbed it briefly before stepping away. "I don't think I'd be up to it."

"I completely understand."

"I hate it. I feel so useless just sitting here. But I'm not ready to drive out to the pasture and do some work." He hung up the beagle ornament on the tree and gave it a little tap so that it swayed back and forth.

"You could come back with me. After lunch, we're saddling up and going for a ride around the ranch."

He shook his head. "Not up for that either, I'm afraid. Sorry."

"Don't be sorry. I just hate the idea of you being all alone out here. Why don't you go up to the ranch house and take Daisy? The dogs could use the company. You can still throw a tennis ball with your other hand, right?"

He quirked a smile. "I suppose. I don't want to impose."

"Tire them out. My mother will be in your debt. And you can snag a cream puff from Suze's dessert tray."

"You're giving my guys cream puffs?" Nate shook his head. "I can't wait to give them hell about this."

"My mother has them putting together lunch for the chuck wagon. They're loving it. It's pandemonium in the kitchen right now. Suze is a baker. Regina manages a bar, and Gayle has Cordon Bleu training."

"Maybe this retreat wasn't a bad idea after all," he said. "At least, we're going to eat good these next two weeks."

"I think it's going to be a great time for them and for us." Janice couldn't wait to tell him the next part. "Part of their group session is going to be helping me turn the land behind my retreat center into a dressage ring. I've used the last of the bank's money for supplies."

Nate blew out a sigh. "Damn, you got some balls on you."

"Why?"

"Your daddy is going to shit himself sideways at the dressage crap."

"It's none of his business. I checked my contract. I can build whatever I want on that land as long as my rent is current and I'm not devaluing the property."

"It's going to get interesting, that's for sure. By the way, Frank told me that Jonas might not make it." Nate shrugged like it didn't mean anything to him.

"Don't think of it like that. He's a sick horse, but he's alive. There's no reason why he can't get better."

"I don't want him suffering," Nate said.

She laid her hand on his arm. "He's not. I swear it. Trust me."

After a moment, he nodded. "I do. I probably should go and see him. You can introduce me to the gals on the retreat, too. I want to take their measure, if we're going to have them come out with us at the end of the two weeks."

"Don't scare them off."

"I'll be as meek as a kitten."

Janice glared at him.

"Trust me."

"Are you sure you're up to this?" She bit her lip.

"I sure as hell don't want to be cooped up here all day. I'll be fine. Once you guys take off on your tour of the ranch, I'll take it easy with the dogs."

"I'm so glad you're all right." She hugged him harder this time. He grunted from the impact, but held her against him.

"You're not crying again, are you?" he asked.

"No, you asshole." Janice wiped a few tears as she let him go.

"I love it when you sweet-talk me." And then he covered her mouth with a quick kiss.

Janice sagged into his arms. He was all right.

Chapter Twelve

THE WEEKEND PASSED by in a blur. Her retreat gals were getting into the swing of ranch life. They had gone fishing on Sunday afternoon, but Donovan put the kibosh on camping out until the hog problem was better under control. Luckily, the hogs had been scarce on the ranch tour and in the pastures where the cows were.

The women were excited about building the dressage ring, too. Most of them had always wanted to try it and the couple that had never ridden before thought it was a better place to start than barrel racing. Janice agreed. She loved the hell out of barrel racing, but she didn't know the first thing about teaching it. Dressage, however, had always had a place in her heart since she was a little girl. Kelly was the rodeo queen, but Janice had USDF gold medals and plaques with her and her winning horses pictured on them. They were still packed away with her things from Kentucky. She should display them at the retreat if this was going to be part of her curriculum.

"Janice," Nate hollered, coming over to her even before she got off the porch of the ranch house. Kelly and Alissa were feeding the dogs for her and her mother was in the kitchen cleaning up. Janice had wanted to stay and help, but they shooed her out the door.

Nate looked handsome and grumpy this morning. His arm was out of the sling and he had been itching to go out with the ranch hands today, but he had promised her father that he'd take her to the auction. That was probably why he looked like he had a bee in his Stetson.

"I'm almost ready," she said. "I've just got to check and make sure that Rita and Melanie know where we're going." Melanie was an Uber driver, so it fit that she would help them carpool to the auction.

"I understand it's not your job to do a bed check, but can you please try to keep your girls out of my ranch hands' beds?"

"What?" Janice asked.

Kelly peeked her head out the doorway. "What's going on?"

"Nothing," they both said in unison.

"Are we running a love connection?" Kelly teased, leaning against the doorjamb. Janice could hear Alissa and her mother singing in the kitchen.

"No, we're not," Janice said, scowling.

Nate led her away by the arm before things could escalate. "Sam wasn't at breakfast today, so I went looking for him. He and the redhead were buck naked in his bunk."

"That's Heidi. Doesn't Sam share a room with Diego, though?"

"Guess where Diego spent the night?"

Janice stopped dead in her tracks. "You're kidding?" He

must have spent it with Tracie, who was Heidi's roommate.

"No. And while I don't give a damn who's banging who, I can't have it affecting my ranch hands' jobs."

"Did Diego make it to breakfast?"

"That's not the point," Nate growled.

"Seems to me, Sam is ruining it for everyone and that's his problem. Not mine." Janice stepped in closer to him. She was glad Nate was feeling better. He was still a little ornery and he moved more stiffly than he usually did, but he and his horse Jonas were slowly on the mend. "Look, I'll mention it to my guys, just so they'll get out of bed in time, but your guys are adults. They know their own schedules."

Nate grunted. "You should have seen it. Beer cans and condoms everywhere."

"Sounds like fun. What are you doing tonight?" She rubbed his good arm and batted her eyelashes at him.

Nate looked around. "Jeez Louise, Janice. Keep it down. You want your father to hear you?"

"He and Esteban are with Donovan at Dillinger pasture, checking for hogs."

"I should be there with them or with the ranch hands."

"Emily needs the experience if she's going to take over for Dad, and you shouldn't fire a rifle with your shoulder still healing."

"You sound like your father."

"There's no reason to get nasty with me. He and I had words the other day and I'm avoiding him like the plague."

Nate's gaze narrowed on her. "About us?"

"Huh? No. About how he treats his cattle. And what

about us, anyway?" She crossed her arms and glared at him. He had better not be waffling again. She'd rip his good arm out of the socket.

"He's not going to be too happy that we're together."

"He's never happy." She rolled her eyes. "But I hear you. I don't want to listen to him get all riled up either."

"I don't like lying to him. Not after all he's done for me."

"After all he's done for you? Nate, this ranch wouldn't even be here, if it wasn't for you."

He gave her a crooked smile. "I appreciate that, but I think he'd like to see you married to someone…better than me."

She snorted. "Shows what he knows. Anyway, him finding out that we're lovers is the least of my worries right now. And it should be the least of his. We've got bills to pay. People on the ranch and cows to move. Not to mention he's on my ass still about becoming a large-animal vet, yet he won't listen to me when I tell him that he's moving the cows too often. They're fatigued from the pace."

"He's worried about the pastures."

"They're already stripped. That's why we're buying so much hay. Anyway, I'll tell you more on the drive. Go get the truck, so we can get going."

Nate blew out a great big sigh.

"And try not to sound so enthusiastic about it."

Janice was going to make sure Nate had a relaxing, fun day, even if it killed them.

He drove the truck to the retreat center and was waiting

impatiently for her as she gave instructions to Rita and Melanie on where to park. Janice was sure he was about to blow the horn at her when she turned around and gave him an evil look. Nate held up his hands in surrender and put the brim of his hat over his eyes.

After she was done a few minutes later, she hauled herself into his truck. "Do you want me to drive?"

"Hell no," he said, setting his hat back to where it normally was.

Up close, he looked more drawn and tired than he had a few minutes ago. She wondered if he was pushing it, but she knew better than to suggest that to him. Janice poured him a cup of coffee from her Thermos and passed it over to him.

"Thank you," he grumbled.

"Where's Daisy?" He usually didn't leave her at home.

"She's not feeling well. Been lethargic and pukey."

"I hope nothing's wrong."

"She probably just got into something she shouldn't have."

"I'll come by and take a look at her later, after lights out at the retreat."

"Thanks."

"Maybe, we can pick up where we left off. Provided you don't go out and get another concussion the next day."

"I'd like to avoid another head injury," he said.

She noticed that he didn't mention the other part. The good part. And she wondered if that was significant or if he was just being dense. "I haven't seen much of you since you got hurt. It doesn't look like you've been taking it easy. That arm should still be in a sling."

"I'm all right. I've been shadowing Emily and giving her some tips."

Janice snickered. "I bet she loved that."

"She doesn't give me grief, unlike some people." Nate smirked at her. "How is the boohoo club coming along?"

"Please don't call it that. It's bad enough I live in fear that my father is going to blurt that out in front of the group. I don't need to worry about you, too."

"All right, don't get your panties in a twist."

Janice waited until he took a big sip of coffee. "I'm not wearing panties."

Choking, Nate turned to her. "Are you out of your mind?"

"Nobody has to know, but you and me." Janice felt a surge of triumph at his expression.

"No one else better know," he muttered.

"How's your head?"

"Which one?"

"The one that got dragged all over Bushwacker pasture." She shifted a little closer to him. "Although, I could check the other one if you want." Janice tickled her fingers up his thigh.

"You're in a feisty mood," he drawled.

She leaned her cheek on his shoulder. "I'm feeling pretty good about things. The retreat is going well. The women are doing great with the teamwork projects Rita has given them and they're really taking ownership of the dressage ring."

"What's Frank got to say about that?"

"He hasn't stopped by and I haven't told him, but we're going to start doing practice rides with Synergy and Black Dahlia by the end of the week."

Nate made a face. "Do you think it's wise to put newbies on those high-strung monsters?"

"They'll be fine. I'll be leading them around until they're settled and feel comfortable."

"The riders or the horses?"

"Both. We're not going to do any jumps. Just basic commands. The horses need the practice and exercise anyway." She slowly stroked her hand up and down his jean-clad thigh. The denim was soft and warm over the hard muscles of his leg.

Nate slung his arm around her as they drove. "Your father wants you to chat up Pete today."

"We're not buying any cattle," she said.

"I know that and you know that."

"And Emily knows that," Janice piped up. "So, that should be the end of that."

"Still…" He took his arm away to make a turn. She missed it when he didn't put it back. "I promised your father you'd at least get Pete's opinion on some of the cattle there."

"Fine. I'll see if I can pick his brain about keeping our cattle healthier. Maybe I'll invite him for dinner this week."

Nate's jaw clenched. "That's a good idea," he said in a tone that sounded like it was anything but.

"He's a bachelor. I'm sure he'd jump at the chance to have a home-cooked meal and it would get my father off my case. You don't think that's manipulative, do you?"

"No." Nate opened his mouth to say something else, but closed it.

Janice knew that when he had something on his mind, it would eventually come out. So, she didn't push him about it. She dug into her purse and checked her to-do list. It was still two pages long, but she was crossing things off at a good pace.

"I'm hoping to camp out one night and cook some meals by the campfire. I want to do baked potatoes in the fire and maybe a pot of baked beans. I've got to pick up some bourbon and mustard." She tapped the end of her pencil against her teeth as she wondered if it would be cheating to buy store-bought biscuits instead of making them from scratch.

"What's Donovan say about the hogs?"

"We're not going to go too far away from the retreat. I had originally wanted to camp by the pond and catch some fish for dinner."

"I wouldn't, unless someone in your group knows how to use a rifle and even then, I'd sleep in the back of my pickup." He jerked a thumb toward the back.

"If you put a mattress in there, maybe we could go to a drive-in. I think there's one in Medina Valley."

"What's playing?" he asked.

"Who cares?" Janice put her hand on his knee and squeezed.

"You're asking for it," he warned.

"Nate, I'll beg for it." Janice pitched her voice low and sexy. She was delighted when he swallowed hard.

"You'll beg all right," he answered.

Now, it was her turn to swallow hard.

They parked in the crowded lot and Janice knew he wouldn't risk a kiss. Nate hated gossip and she was sure that he didn't want her dad to find out about them this way. As they waited for Melanie and Rita to catch up with them, Janice asked, "So when do you want to tell my father?"

Nate didn't say anything. He glared at something over her head.

"Because if you don't mind, I'd rather wait until after Christmas. It's not that I want to hide anything. I just don't want to deal with him until after the stress of the holidays and this retreat is under my belt."

He looked relieved. "I think that's a good idea."

"Great," she said, sagging against the truck. "I was worried your feelings would be hurt."

"No, I'm good. You could never hurt me."

"I never want to," she said, but when she stepped in closer, he stepped away and said, "Pete! Over here."

Janice resisted the urge to groan.

"How are you guys doing?" Pete came over just as Rita and the retreat women joined them.

"Everybody, this is the Three Sisters Ranch's veterinarian, Pete Dickerson." Janice introduced Tracie, Suze, Regina, Gayle, Heidi and Melanie to him. "And you know Rita."

"I do." Doc Pete actually blushed.

Janice elbowed Nate behind their backs as they were walking into the auction.

"What?" he said, crankily.

"Did you see that?" she whispered.

"No."

"I think Doc Pete is sweet on Rita."

"Really?" Nate seemed to perk up at that. "He's a good catch. Rich doctor."

Janice snorted. "Rita's a good catch, too. She's a brilliant therapist and owns her own business. Don't be such a sexist pig. Money isn't everything in a relationship."

"It is, if you don't have any," he said, grimly. He pushed his way through the crowd to the beer tent. She let him be. It was his day to relax. He might as well sit in the shade with a beer, even if it was only ten o'clock in the morning.

Oh well. It was five o'clock somewhere.

Sighing, Janice joined her group and gave them a quick tour of the stockades and talked about what made buying cattle profitable and what to look for. The hay and manure tickled her nose, but a few of the women looked sick to their stomachs.

"You'll get used to the smell after a while," Janice said.

"I don't want to get used to it." Gayle wandered over toward the beer tent.

Janice felt a slight flutter of jealousy, but Gayle didn't pay any attention to Nate. Janice couldn't understand why she didn't at least flirt with him. He was easily the most handsome man there. Nate was leaning back in his chair, listening to a rancher she didn't recognize.

Walking farther by the pens, Janice pointed out the traits to look for in buying cattle and what to watch out for. They stopped in front of a pen that had two nice-looking Angus cows.

"These guys are real beauties," Pete said.

Janice agreed. Biting her lip, she wondered how much she could get them for. It was harder than she had thought to be here without the intention to buy. It was like going to a bakery just to look.

In another pen, a brown-and-white spotted longhorn cow and her snow-white calf were chewing their cud. Rita and Suze cooed over the baby. It was kind of cute.

"We should be having some calves soon," Janice said. "Pete, are you going to be around in a few weeks."

"Should be," he said, giving the cow and her calf the once-over. "Are you interested in these guys?"

Janice shrugged. "They look good to me."

Pete flashed his credentials and the attendant let him in. Pete checked the hooves and the ears and noses. She could have done that too, but then she would want to buy them. It was hard enough resisting the snowy-faced calf that had come close to the fence.

"Are you going to go it alone for the births?" he asked.

"I'd like you there with me," she said. She could do it in a pinch, but she would rather assist him.

"I'll tell you what—I'll observe and if you need me, I'll step in. If not, no charge."

That should please her father, but it made her feel a bit guilty. "We can pay you for your time," she said.

"How about in trade?"

Suze and Regina nudged each other and giggled.

"What type of trade are you suggesting?" Rita said, a little frostily.

"Sarah Sullivan makes the best lasagna on the planet."

And since the women had already sampled it, they had to agree. While they were waxing poetic about her mother's lasagna, Janice walked back to the Angus cows that had caught her eye.

"Are you going to bid on them?" Suze asked.

"If my father had his say, we would come home with a few cattle. But we didn't bring the trailer. Once you buy them, you have to take them home the same day."

"Couldn't you borrow a trailer?" Regina asked.

"I brought one today," Pete said.

"But you don't have any cows," Janice said.

"I know, but I always like to be prepared."

Rita smirked. "Yeah, you're a regular Boy Scout."

"We'd love to see you bid and win," Melanie said.

"Well, it is exciting," Janice admitted. "But we'd have to quarantine the cattle for ten days to make sure they are healthy."

"But if you bought one, we could take care of it for most of those ten days."

"Uh," Janice said. It was a good idea, and what better way to get them involved? On the other hand, Emily would kill her and they didn't have the money. Or did they? Depending how the bidding went, they might get the cows for a good price. And maybe if they bought them for a quick resale in the spring, they could turn a profit.

"Please?" Tracie said.

"Let me call my sister." Janice walked away from them

and took out her cell phone. She hated to dim the group's enthusiasm. She knew there was nothing like the excitement of an auction that you had a stake in.

"What's up?" Emily asked, her voice sounding hollow as if she was speaking through a wind tunnel.

"Call me crazy, but can we afford two Anguses?"

"What happened to just going there to look?"

"I know. I know. I'm the only person in the world to impulse-purchase cows." Janice went back and took two photos, one of the Angus cows and one of the longhorn and her baby. "What do you think of them?"

"I really want to say yes," Emily said. "But it would stretch us too thin and we wouldn't see a profit in time to make a difference. Are you mad at me?"

"I'm proud of you. Last year, you would have green-lighted it and maxed out our cards."

"To be fair, my card is already maxed," Emily said with a half chuckle.

"I still have some room on mine," Janice said. "And Christmas is coming up. Should we get Dad a pair of Angus cows for Christmas?"

"I was thinking new boots and a pair of overalls. That's more our budget. Unless, of course, you can sweet-talk Pete into buying them for you."

Janice snorted. "Why would Pete buy us cows?"

"Not us, dummy. You."

"Why me?"

"Because some men buy women flowers and diamond bracelets. Other men buy more practical things."

Janice looked over at Pete, who waved to her. Since the auction wasn't going on, she felt free to wave back. But she had to remind the group not to do that once the auctioneer got going. "Why do you think he'd buy me a gift like that? We're not dating."

"You could be," Emily said. "I've seen the way he looks at you."

"At me? No, at Rita."

"No, at you."

"Oh shit," Janice said. She hoped she hadn't been leading Pete on. He was a nice man. A good-looking one, but she'd finally got Nate into bed and she wasn't going to give that up without a fight.

"Oh shit? He's handsome, rich, owns his own business, and loves animals. You're perfect for each other. And did I mention he's rich?"

"Money doesn't buy happiness," Janice said through numbed lips.

"No, but it does keep ranches out of bankruptcy. Why don't you bat your eyes at him and see if he'll buy you some cows? Because that's the only way we're going to get any today. Do you hear me?"

"I hear you," Janice said. "But I wish I hadn't."

Chapter Thirteen

NATE COULDN'T LEAVE the dinner table fast enough. Not even Sarah's cheesecake could keep him lingering over coffee. He couldn't decide if he wanted to punch Pete in the face or be thankful that he was helping the Three Sisters Ranch out.

Not only did the rich veterinarian buy the two Angus cows and the longhorn cow and calf that Janice had her heart set on, he was housing the cows at the Three Sisters Ranch. Pete was now paying rent and upkeep to have Janice and her retreat take care of the cows for him. Because he could. Because buying cows was as expensive to Pete as buying a six-pack of Budweiser was to Nate. Who impulse-bought cows? Someone who was trying to impress a girl, that's who. Nate shook his head in disgust and a little bit of envy.

Frank was over the moon.

Janice was giddy.

Pete was humble.

Nate was leaning toward punching his lights out. He fed Daisy and gave her fresh water, but noticed she barely touched the food he'd given her this morning. Hopefully, she'd be better tomorrow when they were back on the trail.

So would he.

Glaring at the little tree that Janice had put up, he resisted the urge to kick it down. It shouldn't bother him. He thought he was over all these feelings of resentment and anger a long time ago. But there was something about this year that made him commiserate with Ebenezer Scrooge.

He was probably just tired, like the ER doc said. Rubbing a hand over his face, Nate tamped down frustrated feelings. All he'd been doing these past few days was taking it easy and the longer he was gone from work, the sooner the Sullivans would realize that they didn't really need him after all. Esteban could step in. Or Doc Pete.

Suddenly it felt like the walls of the cottage were closing in on him. Nate stormed out and walked down to the barn to check on Jonas. Unfortunately, that took him by the pasture where the new arrivals were being held in quarantine. They were good stock and an excellent addition to anyone's herd. Doc Pete didn't have a herd. He had bought the cows for Janice. He was keeping them here to help the family.

Pete was their best hope for keeping the Three Sisters Ranch running until Emily could build up her wind farm. Nate needed to step away from Janice. And if he was a real friend, he'd play matchmaker, like her father wanted him to. But right now, with the sting of Christmas in the back of his throat, it was too much to ask of him.

Jonas nickered softly as Nate came in the barn. The horse felt a little cold, so Nate draped a blanket over him.

"How you doing, boy?"

Nate patted him and his nerves settled a bit. Grabbing a

stool, he sat down in the pen and combed through his mane. Jonas liked the extra attention and it soothed Nate almost as much as it did the horse. However, when it was time to leave, Nate felt the memories creeping in like shadows.

His father had lost him in a game of poker.

Nate stared up at the moon and let the truth of it settle over him. It wasn't the first time he'd acknowledged it and he thought he'd put these feelings to bed a long time ago, but here they were again.

It could have been worse. His father could have lost him to a man with proclivities that would have put Nate in danger. Instead, the man who'd won him in a poker game brought him home, fed him a good meal, let him take a nice hot shower and sleep in a soft, warm bed. The next day had been Christmas, and even though the man's family couldn't have been expecting him, there were a few presents under the tree for him. He still had the Cody Hart belt buckle somewhere. There had also been sweaters and a decent set of boots that Nate hadn't cared were obvious hand-me-downs.

In the chaos of that Christmas where cousins, aunts and uncles came in and out through the day, no one seemed surprised to find one more kid. He had spent the day eating everything he could get his hands on and playing Nintendo games. It was the best damned Christmas of his life.

Until that night.

His father had broken into the house and robbed the family blind, forcing Nate to be quiet and hitting him hard when he had protested.

"Did you think you were going to stay here forever?" his fa-

ther had sneered. "You're just another mouth to feed and they're glad to be rid of you."

"But you lost. Fair and square."

That had earned him another backhand.

"He took you to make a point. He didn't really want you. Sooner or later, you would have pissed him off and he'd have kicked you out. Then, where would you be? Let's go. This should keep us living in style for a while."

And it had. They joined up with a traveling rodeo and when that went bust, they worked as ranch hands all over Texas until his father dropped dead.

He had been as skittish as a colt, that first Christmas at the Three Sisters Ranch. Nate hadn't known how to turn his boss down when he invited him for dinner. He'd been terrified that he would use the wrong fork at the dinner table or something. But it hadn't been like that at all.

Nate had brought Sarah a Christmas cactus and Frank a bottle of Jim Beam. Both presents had earned him brownie points. He had gotten the girls gift cards to the local nail salon and they were thrilled. They ate a big meal, played a few board games and watched football. When Sarah and Frank started dozing off on the couch, he and the girls went out riding.

He hadn't been able to sleep that night. He kept waiting for the other shoe to drop. Logically, he knew his dead drunk father wasn't going to show up and rip him away from his new life—not that he would have let him anyway. But Nate thought, for sure, the next day Frank would tell him it had all been a big mistake.

But he hadn't.

And the next Christmas it had been the same, as well as the year after that, and the one after that.

Except now, it was getting awfully crowded in the ranch house. Kelly and Trent, Emily and Donovan, Janice and Pete. Nate didn't want to be a pity guest. He should start looking for places to go so they didn't feel obligated to invite him this year.

He supposed he shouldn't have been surprised when he saw Janice waiting for him on his steps. She had a slice of cheesecake on a plate, and she was petting a sulking Daisy.

"I think she might be running a fever," Janice said.

"She hasn't been eating well." Nate crouched down. "She doesn't look good to me."

"I'll give her a full check-up tomorrow," she said. "I'll get a fecal sample too and see if Doc Pete can test it."

"He's just a regular knight in shining armor, isn't he?" Nate said, walking into the house.

She followed, holding the door open for Daisy to take her time walking in. "She's lethargic," Janice said. "I don't like that. You should have told me. I would have had Pete take a look at her."

Pete again. Was there anything he couldn't do?

Nate grunted.

"It is weird," he admitted. Daisy was a very high-energy dog. "I'm hoping she'll bounce back tomorrow. If she doesn't, can you look her over?"

"Sure."

"It will be good to get back into the routine."

"Are you sure you're both up to it? You seem a little off, too." Janice put the plate on the table.

"Am I running a fever?"

She placed a cool hand on his forehead. "You seem hot to me. Maybe you should take your clothes off and lie down.

He had to chuckle and before he could stop himself, he wrapped his arm around her and brought her in for a kiss. She tasted tart, like a lemon cheesecake, and the way her body molded into his was just as delicious. He could kiss her for hours, and right now that was all he wanted to do. He didn't want to think about her and Doc Pete or her father's expectations. She had come to him, and if she was thinking about dating the veterinarian, she wouldn't have been kissing him back so enthusiastically.

If that one shining Christmas of his youth had taught him anything, it was to enjoy the good things while they lasted, because with a spin of the wheel, it could all change for the worse. Nate let her unbutton his shirt because he liked the feel of her hands over his chest. When she went for his belt buckle, the little voice of his conscience tried to reason with him.

You're only going to get hurt.

Nate told that sumbitch to take a hike. Janice could have chosen to stay with Doc Pete. She came to Nate instead, and he didn't have it in him to turn her away. Leading her into the bedroom, shucking off clothes the whole way, Nate was thrilled to feel her naked body against his.

Janice pushed him down on the bed and clambered on top of him. He tangled his fingers though her hair and kissed her thoroughly. The little sounds she was making in the back of her throat drove him a little wild and when she rolled off him and grabbed his cock, Nate nearly went off in her hand. She stroked him fast. Nate wrenched his mouth away.

"Slow down," he groaned. "We've got all night."

He released her hair when she started kissing down his chest. "Fast now. Slow later."

"Whatever you want, darlin'."

She took him deep in her mouth.

"Whatever you want."

His fingers gripped the sheets as wave after wave of pleasure pulsed through him. She was making rational thought impossible. How could he have stayed away from her all these years? Janice was everything he ever wanted in a woman, a wife, a partner. Nate was going to explode if her sweet mouth didn't stop bringing him to the brink.

"Come here, sweetheart. I want to touch you." He urged her back up to his mouth and indulged himself in running his hands up and down her body.

Janice shivered and hooked her leg over his hip. Nate could feel her wet heat just inches from his cock and it was all he could do to stop himself from sliding inside her. Cupping her breasts, he sucked hard on one nipple and then the other. Now it was her turn to clutch her fingers through his hair and hold his head. She arched against him.

"Please, Nate. Now."

"Come first," he said and slid his fingers through her soft folds.

She threw back her head and moaned while he flicked

and tickled her clit. Her thighs clamped down on his hand and she pumped her hips as she rode out her orgasm. Janice shook and cried out his name.

"Perfect," he said, kissing down her belly.

"Nate, now."

"Let me taste you first." Nate parted her eager thighs and licked her slowly. She shivered and quaked.

"Nate," she whispered.

He tongued her faster, looking into her beautiful eyes.

Mine.

Yanking her hips to his mouth, he kissed her deeply and intimately, making love to her with his thrusting tongue and greedy lips. She wasn't his. Not completely. But for tonight, for every night until he was forced to acknowledge she wasn't, he was going to treat her as if she was.

Humming in pleasure, Nate enjoyed having Janice writhing and panting underneath him. She shrieked when she came and he barely pulled away in time to put on the condom before she pushed him flat on his back and straddled his hips.

She rode him hard, bouncing deep. Nate held on to her ass and enjoyed the view of her luscious breasts bouncing and her wide-open mouth moaning incoherently. His entire body was strung on the edge of pleasure and absolute abandonment of his senses. Nate couldn't delay his orgasm any longer. He came so completely, he nearly went blind. But Janice wasn't there yet and rocked on him, their bodies slapping together in a loud rhythm that kept him hard. He would do anything for her. She was his entire world.

Nate nearly told her that, nearly begged for her to stay with him. But he wasn't that far gone. Not yet. Hopefully not ever. He loved her, though. Loved her so damn much.

"Nate," Janice cried, shaking apart. She collapsed against him and he rolled them on their sides, still joined together. Clamping down on him and then releasing him, Janice sunk her teeth into his shoulder.

Now, it was his turn to cry out. But not in pain. Deep pleasure and satisfaction washed over him at the dazed and wild look in her eyes. He kissed her, holding her tight against him until their breathing came back to normal. Sliding out of her, he took care of the condom and then came right back to bed. Getting under the covers, he wrapped himself around her.

"Stay with me, tonight," he said.

"I can't," she said regretfully. "My parents know I'm here and if I don't come home…" She trailed off.

Nate closed his eyes so she wouldn't see the frustration in them. She was right, of course. Frank would lose his shit.

"It's just until the new year," she said, pressing worried kisses along his brow. "I just want a drama-free Christmas."

Frank wanted her to marry another man. But that was drama for another day.

"I know," he said, not wanting to think any more about that. There had to be a way around it. He was just too tired to figure it out.

"But I can stay for a little bit." She rested her head on his chest.

He stroked her back, while she entangled her legs against

his. This was nice too.

The sound of Daisy retching broke him out of the haze of bliss. Welcome back to reality.

"Poor little girl," Janice murmured.

"I'll be right back," he said wryly.

"Put on the light so you don't step in it."

Nate smirked. "Good idea." He flicked on the bedside lamp and when he turned around, he saw Daisy shaking on the floor next to a puddle. "It's all right, girl," he said, crouching down beside her. Then he froze. "Is that blood?"

Janice scrambled out of bed. Daisy whimpered when Nate ran his hand down the dog's side.

"Is that tinsel?" Janice said, pointing.

Nate cursed and got dressed quickly. Janice called Pete, and luckily, he hadn't left the ranch house yet.

"Pete, I think Nate's dog ate some tinsel and it's causing her some distress." Janice deliberately kept it vague to keep him from worrying but it wasn't fooling Nate a bit. He knew his dog. She had been sick all this time and he hadn't taken it seriously. He felt terrible.

"I'm taking her to Honeyman," Nate said, picking Daisy up as gently as he could.

Janice hung up on Pete and got dressed as well. Nate was already out the door.

"Wait for me," she said, hopping on one foot to get her boot on. "I'll drive and you can hold her."

"Hurry up," Nate snarled.

"I'm sorry," she said. "This is all my fault. You said you didn't want a tree and now Daisy is sick because of it. I'm so sorry."

Nate couldn't answer her. His heart was in his throat. This couldn't be happening. First Jonas. Now Daisy. The keys for the truck were already in the ignition and Janice hopped in the truck and drove as fast as she could without jostling the poor little dog. Pete was waiting for them in his car and followed them to Honeyman Veterinary Hospital.

NATE OWED PETE Dickerson big.

This was gearing up to be his worst Christmas since he was a kid. His horse was recovering from being bitten by a snake and his dog was recovering from surgery where the tinsel she had eaten had caused a blockage in her intestines.

Needless to say, after they got home from the vet hospital late last night, the tree that Janice had put up in his house was moved to the retreat center and safe from all the dogs for the time being.

He hadn't bothered going to sleep because he'd have to be up in a few hours. He couldn't take Janice's apologies anymore. She was wrung out and distraught, having assisted Pete in the surgery. It wasn't her fault and he certainly didn't blame her.

Nate had wanted to ease her feelings, but he was afraid if he tried, he'd come apart. Instead, he worked a long day in the saddle, skipping lunch to take a siesta in the truck. He hadn't been hungry anyway. When they got back tonight, he forced himself to have dinner with the ranch hands and he felt slightly more human after a burger and fries. He had planned on face-planting into his bed, the bed that he and Janice had shared what seemed like a lifetime ago.

But before he could, Frank had knocked on his door.

"Nate? Got a minute?"

Nate wanted to refuse. He didn't have it in him to get into it with the old man. Not after his last twenty-four hours. But he was also too tired to argue.

"Yeah," he said, letting him in. "You want a beer?"

"I wouldn't say no to a cold one."

Nate opened up two Rahr extra darks and handed him one.

"How's the pup?"

"She survived the surgery." Nate looked at the text that Pete had sent him. "She's going to need to stay at the hospital a few days to make sure there's no infection. But she'll pull through."

"Pete's a good doctor."

Nate nodded, too raw to think about how much he owed the vet. "Janice helped, too. You would have been proud of her."

"I'm proud of them both. I wanted to tell you that was good work finagling it so Pete bought her the cows."

Holding up his hands, Nate said, "I had nothing to do with it. That was all his idea."

"She was impressed, right?"

"I was impressed." Nate took a long swig of his beer.

"What's our next step?"

"Our next step is to butt the hell out." Nate was pretty

sure he didn't sound as vicious as he felt.

"I want you to go to the parade with them on Friday and find a way to get them together."

"Fuck no." Yeah, that time it slipped out. Nate would rather be slathered in barbecue sauce and staked out for the fire ants. "I've got a job to do and it's not playing match-maker for your daughter and the rich doctor."

"Esteban can handle the work for the day. Your doctor wanted you to take it easy, right?"

Nate snorted. "Now, you're all for listening to the doctor's orders? You take her to the parade."

"I'm already going. Sarah's on the parade committee. I'm going to have my hands full with that. Trent, Kelly and Alissa are going to be riding in the parade, too. The bull-riding school's got a float. Donovan and Emily are manning the booths for the riding school and the safari tours. That leaves you."

"Frank, are you sure you want this? I mean Pete's a good guy. He's a regular saint, but I don't know if he has Janice's heart." *Mostly because I want it.*

Frank's eyes narrowed on him and Nate wondered if he'd gone too far.

"Something you want to tell me?"

Nate grit his teeth. "I'd marry her. I'm not rich. But I…" He was not about to tell her father that he loved her. Janice deserved to hear it first. "I think she and I could be happy. If we worked hard, we could keep the ranch going."

He braced for the explosion, but none came. Frank looked at him thoughtfully. "If I thought you could make each other happy, I'd be all for it. But you're too much like me. Too angry. Too set in your ways. I'd hate to see you and Janice make a go of it and then wind up hating each other."

"I could never hate her." That much he could tell Frank.

"You might not have noticed, but I haven't been the best dad," Frank said, finishing his beer. "You got anything stronger?"

Nate fished out a bottle of whiskey and poured them each two fingers.

"You were better than mine." Nate sighed.

"I almost lost Kelly. And Alissa. All because I was too stubborn. I drove Janice away. Hell, Emily had to go to Africa to get away from me. I had good intentions. I only wanted what was best for them. But they rebelled. They refused to see it my way."

"I'd like to think I'm not the 'my way or the highway' type," Nate said.

"Well, you are. Just ask any of your ranch hands."

"That's the ranch hands. Not my…" he almost said family, but he changed it to "…friends."

"Janice needs a husband who shares her interests and understands her."

"Like Emily and Donovan?" Nate quipped. Emily was a vegetarian and Donovan was a trophy hunter.

"They compromised. He gave up his hunting lodge for a nature safari."

"But he still hunts boar and deer."

"When he needs to. He doesn't have hunters come in anymore because it upsets Emily. I couldn't do that. If it were up to me, Emily would just have to deal with it. You're the same way."

Nate shifted uncomfortably. Maybe, he should have pushed back at a few of Frank's opinions. He had never wanted to rock the boat and find himself out of a job. What Frank was saying, though, touched a nerve. Nate *had* advised Donovan to keep booking hunting parties, even though it distressed Emily to think of the animals being killed for sport. "Janice isn't Emily."

"Do you know what Emily wants to do?"

"I know she's got a lot of ideas."

"She wants us to get out of the beef business."

A flare of alarm ran through him. "What?"

"She wants to have dairy cows instead."

"This isn't a dairy farm," Nate said. Dairy farms didn't need ranch hands or a ranch foreman. Where did that leave him? Out of a job and out of the only family he'd ever really known. He drew in a shaky sigh.

"Janice is going to side with her. You're going to side with me. And we're not going to give in. What do you think that's going to do to your relationship?"

Nate opened his mouth, but no words came so he just drank his whiskey.

"They're going to sell our cattle and use the money to put up a dairy barn and buy the equipment and milk cows. Emily says it's too expensive to have Angus and longhorns. But that's bullshit. The real reason she wants to sell our beef is because Emily thinks having dairy cows is more humane." Frank sneered the last two words. "Over my dead body."

"Frank," Nate said warningly because Frank was starting to lose his temper.

"But if Janice marries Pete, Emily's argument that it's too expensive goes away. Janice and Pete will be our vets. We can buy a dairy barn to keep Emily happy and you and I can continue with our cattle." Frank emptied his whiskey and set his glass down with a clank. "I'm glad we had this talk."

Nate's head was whirling more than it was after Jonas had dragged him halfway across Bushwacker pasture.

"So you'll escort Janice to the parade on Friday and help keep the boohoo club occupied while she and Doc Pete get to know each other better."

"I'm not sure…"

"I'm not asking, boy. We'll talk later." Frank let himself out while Nate just stared after him. He poured himself another whiskey.

"It's official," Nate said to the empty room. "Christmas blows."

It was too empty in his house without Daisy and he couldn't relax after the conversation he'd just had with Frank, so he wandered over to the retreat center. The lights were on in Janice's makeshift dressage ring and he saw that Black Dahlia and Synergy were being put through their paces.

Janice was watching from the sidelines, looking a little twitchy. But her horses were following directions, even though the retreat women obviously weren't comfortable seated on them.

"I hope they're better on the trail horses," he grumbled,

coming up to lean on the fence next to her.

"What are you doing up?" she asked, placing a hand over her heart. "Is it Daisy?"

"As far as I know, she's still at Honeyman recovering. I can pick her up tomorrow. Thank you for assisting Doc Pete when he operated."

"Of course," she said. "It's my fault she was in surgery."

He reached down and gripped her hand. "No, it's not. Daisy just ate something she shouldn't."

"You told me not to put up the tree. I should have listened. I'm so sorry."

"Don't feel guilty," he said. "She's going to be all right." It was odd that he was comforting her about this. After all, she'd helped save Daisy's life. "Right?"

"Right." Janice nodded. "She needs to rest and heal up. Just like you did. Would you let her stay with my mom during the day? She'll keep her isolated from the other dogs, but that way Daisy won't be all alone."

"I'd appreciate that," he said.

"Pete's a miracle worker," Janice said. "He was so calm and he knew just what to do."

"He's a good man," Nate admitted. And now he owed him. If Pete wanted Janice, Nate should do the right thing and step away. "You and he made a good team."

"I was terrified," she said shakily. "If something went wrong in the operation, I never would have been able to forgive myself."

"Shit happens."

"Not at Christmastime," Janice said.

"Especially then." Nate didn't want to get into this right now, but he also didn't want to go back home alone. He watched as Janice switched the women and instructed them on their technique. "How late are you going to be out here with this?"

"About another hour. I need to have them used to handling horses by this time next week."

Nate made a face. "A guaranteed shit show."

"Thanks for the positive outlook." She whirled on him, blinking back tears.

Crap. Frank was right. He was too ornery of a bastard for her. "I'm being a realist. You can't expect someone who has never been on a horse to spend a day in the saddle, in the hot sun, working nonstop."

"They'll be ready," Janice said between her teeth.

If drive and enthusiasm and sheer bullheadedness could get them there, Janice would have it covered. He wanted to ask her about the plan to get rid of the beef cattle and start a dairy farm, but he was afraid she'd confirm what Frank had said. And where would that leave him?

Where does that leave us?

Chapter Fourteen

JANICE KNEW SHE'D screwed up. And even though Daisy was going to pull through, she should have listened to Nate about the Christmas tree. It didn't matter that her heart had been in the right place and that she couldn't stand seeing Nate being so distant and bah-humbug-ish about Christmas. He had his reasons. Reasons he was keeping from her.

Nate hadn't been around a lot the last few days. He went out with the ranch hands in the morning and then went back to his cottage at night. Janice could only hope he was resting his sore shoulder and concentrating on taking care of Daisy.

Gayle and Heidi were doing great roping the wooden sawhorses they were practicing on. Tracie and Regina looked better in the saddle than they had when they first got here. Everyone was settling into ranching life and in between sessions with Rita, they got the dressage ring built enough to do some practice.

Janice had forgotten how much enjoyment she got out of the sport. While Emily took Melanie and Suze over to Trent's bull-riding ring to do some barrel racing, Janice had the rest of the retreat taking turns on Synergy and Black Dahlia, practicing controlling the horses through the patterns. That would help them remember how to move with the horse when they were on the cattle run next week. So far, it looked like the new riders would be joining them. They were going to be sore and she'd probably have them herd from the back, but she was confident they could handle themselves. Even better, Janice could see by their wide grins that they were confident as well.

Her phone rang and she looked down and saw it was Kelly calling her.

"What's up?" she asked, wondering why her sister just didn't text her.

"Some flashy-looking guy in a souped-up Caddy wants to talk to you about renting the retreat center. I told him you were in a lesson right now, but he was willing to wait. How long do you think you're going to be?"

"I can wrap it up, but it's still going to be about a half hour. You can tell him all about it, though. Maybe get his number so I can call him later."

"I did. He still wants to talk with you."

"All right. Ask him if he wants to wait or if he'd rather come back tomorrow."

After a pause, Kelly came back on the phone. "He'll wait. I'll give him a piece of banana bread and a cup of coffee."

Janice finished up the lesson and then instructed the women to take the horses back to the barn and feed and brush them down and then to take it easy until dinner. They were going to cook over an open fire and camp out by the pond tonight. Donovan and Trent had agreed to come along to provide hog protection, so her sisters and Alissa were going to join them.

She wanted to invite Nate, but after everything, she thought he needed a good night's sleep in bed more than he needed to be on the cold hard ground. Wishing she looked a little more presentable for the potential client, Janice combed her fingers through her hair and straightened her clothes as she walked up to her parents' house. Sitting at the kitchen table coloring with Alissa was an older gentlemen with salt and pepper hair. He was handsome in a slick, silver fox sort of way. He rose out of his chair and offered her his hand when she walked in.

"Hi, I'm Janice," she said.

"Charlie Lincoln. Thank you for seeing me. I'm sorry to interrupt your retreat."

"We were taking a break before dinner anyway," Janice said, shaking his hand. Sizing him up, she was pretty sure he wasn't going to slap her ass like the last guy did.

"Your sister tells me that you're taking the group camping tonight."

"We have to watch out for piggies. Daddy is going to keep us safe," Alissa said solemnly.

Janice could have lived without him knowing about the feral hog problem since it was being taken care of, but it didn't seem to faze Charlie. "Would you like a tour?"

"I'd love one."

Leading him outside, she gestured for him to get into the Gator. Starting it up, she took him around the ranch area first, pointing out the heifer pens and the garden. "What type of retreat are you looking to do here?"

"I'm going to be honest with you, Miss Sullivan."

"Janice," she corrected.

"I'm an ex-con."

Janice braked hard and they both lurched ahead. "You might have brought that up before I drove out all alone here with you." She refused to panic. She was in yelling distance and someone would hear her. Although he had been alone with Kelly and Alissa and hadn't tried anything. She shouldn't be so judgmental, but he could have been more forthcoming. The fact that he just showed up on the ranch instead of calling first and being upfront got her back up. Shifting so she could jump out and run easier, she turned to face him.

"I probably should have mentioned it, but people tend to react the way you're doing right now, when I do." He gestured at her tense fight-or-flight posture, but she refused to let her guard down. "I made a lot of bad decisions in my life and people got hurt. But I was in for theft and fraud. I'm not a violent man."

Janice put the Gator back in gear and steered toward the retreat center. She only had his word for that, but she would accept it until she could verify his story. There was no sense just sitting out here in the middle of the ranch. What worried her was she might have shown him where they were camping tonight if he hadn't dropped his bombshell on them. "So why are you telling me this now?"

"It's part of what I'm looking to rent the retreat for. I want to bring ex-cons here."

Yeah, her father would shit a brick sideways. But she

wasn't going to say no until she was back with other people, so she nodded.

"It's hard going back to the real world after doing time and as you can imagine, some may be inclined to go back to old habits and poor choices. I was talking with my parole officer and he thinks it would help with my rehabilitation as well if I continue my mentorship of prisoners."

"How did you find out about my retreat?"

"I've seen some of the ads you've put out."

Janice felt a twinge of conscience. People made mistakes. They deserved a second chance if they were trying to change and had paid for their crimes. Part of her retreat mission statement was to help people be more confident and live their lives to the fullest.

"I wouldn't feel comfortable having violent offenders at the ranch," Janice said, thinking of Alissa and her parents. Still, she couldn't put her family in danger. But would they be in danger if the ex-cons were nonviolent? Janice just wasn't sure.

"Of course not. I would be hosting white-collar criminals, all of whom have served their time and have been deemed safe to be released into society."

Janice chewed her bottom lip. "I would have to bring in extra security." Maybe she could even hire back some of the ranch hands they had let go.

"I completely understand, and I would insist that you add their salaries to my bill. This would be an ongoing contract. Three or four times a year."

Between his groups and Rita's groups, she could have a

comfortable income. She'd be able to contribute to the ranch's debts, pay down her own, and maybe put in some improvements to the dressage ring. "What type of services are you interested in?" she asked.

"Animal therapy."

"I'm not a therapist," Janice said. "But I do have access to one." She wondered if Rita would be interested in offering her services to Charlie's retreat groups.

"That's good to know, but I simply meant having the guests take care of animals. The cows, the other animals. And, of course, fishing, camping, and horseback riding would be paradise for men who have been locked up for a few years."

"What about dressage?" she asked.

Charlie blinked at her. "I'm not quite sure what that is."

"Never mind," she said. "That could come later. How are you planning to pay for the retreat?" She didn't want to take dirty money…if he still even had the money he stole.

Smiling, Charlie said, "I've got some government grants to cover the first five years."

Five years. Janice let out a slow breath. Five years of retreats would give Emily's wind turbines a chance to pay themselves off and start to make a profit. She parked outside of the retreat center. Rita waved at her from the porch where the women were sitting down with a pitcher of iced tea.

"We've got a group here now. The center has four bedrooms and can comfortably sleep eight people, if you have people willing to share the two king-size beds."

"I don't see that happening." Charlie shook his head.

She hid a grin. "The other rooms have two twin beds in them. So you can fit six people."

"Five and me. I'll be staying here during the retreat."

They got out of the Gator and she took him around the house after introducing them to Rita and her group. "They're training to go out on a cattle drive, in addition to learning team-building skills and other confidence boosters."

"This sounds exactly what I'm looking for," Charlie said as they walked around the back of the retreat center where the dressage ring was. "Can you draw up the contracts this week, so we can schedule the first group?"

"I'm going to need to check your references and see your grant paperwork," Janice said, folding her arms in front of her chest.

"Of course. I can email that to you."

She nodded. "I think we can come to an agreement." Out of the corner of her eye, she saw Donovan and Emily on the ATV roaring up toward them.

Charlie tensed next to her.

"That's my sister and her fiancé," Janice said. "He takes care of the feral hogs, so your group wouldn't have to worry about encountering them."

"Fiancé?" Charlie said, weakly.

"Yeah, they're getting married next year after my sister Kelly ties the knot." Janice tried not to feel like she was always going to be a bridesmaid, and never a bride.

Donovan didn't look like he was going to stop and Janice took a cautious step back. Something was wrong. Emily was wide-eyed and white-faced. Launching himself out of the ATV, Donovan looked ready to tackle Charlie, but Emily held his arm back.

"What's going on?" Janice said, looking nervously back at Rita's retreat. They were watching the drama unfold as if it was a reality show.

"What the hell are you doing here?" Donovan asked, low and angry.

"Not what you think," Charlie said, opening his hands in a placating manner.

"You two know each other?" Janice asked.

"Charlie is Donovan's father."

"Oh," Janice said, brightening. That made things easier.

"No," Emily said, shaking her head.

Right. Ex-con. Fraud. Hurt a lot of people.

"Oh," Janice said. That made things a little more difficult.

"Get in the ATV," Donovan said to Charlie.

Nodding, Charlie turned and held out his hand to Janice. She shook it automatically. "I'll send you the information you requested as soon as I get back to my motel room."

"Don't trust a damn thing he says," Donovan said, grabbing his father by the arm and tugging him away.

"By all means, you should have Donovan vet my documentation. This is a real offer," Charlie said, shaking free and getting into the passenger side of the ATV.

Donovan pressed his lips together and drove away without another word.

"He's not a good man," Emily said.

"He seems like he wants to make amends for that." Janice was relieved that Rita's group seemed to have lost interest and were excitedly getting ready for the camping trip.

"Donovan doesn't trust him."

"Do you?"

"I've never met him. I went with Donovan to visit him in prison once. He seems to want to have a relationship with his son, but Donovan doesn't want a damn thing to do with him."

"That does complicate things."

"Complicate them? Why? He lied to get in here."

"No, he didn't." Janice explained what Charlie had proposed.

"Dad will never go for it. Nate won't either."

That got Janice's back up. "Well, then it's a good thing it's not their decision."

Chapter Fifteen

C AMPING THAT NIGHT was a little tense. Donovan was scowling and glaring at her across the campfire and Trent looked really uncomfortable settling in with his bad leg. Janice was sure if it hadn't been for how excited Alissa was, they would have called it a night after the s'mores were gone.

As she watched people get zipped up into their tents, she was relieved that Emily convinced Donovan to turn in with her instead of staying up to put out the fire. She didn't relish having an argument with him way out here. She hadn't made up her mind about his father's retreat yet. If he was running a scam, she was confident Donovan could ferret it out. But Janice had talked to Charlie's parole officer a few hours ago and everything seemed legitimate.

She could understand his concerns, but Donovan and her family had to realize that she wouldn't do anything to endanger them. They had to trust her as much as they were trusting Emily with her wind turbines.

As she was banking down the fire for the night, she heard a few muffled giggles and out of the corner of her eye saw Diego and Sam ducking into Heidi and Tracie's individual tents.

"Oh, honestly." Janice shook her head. Once the food was stored in airtight coolers and the fire was completely out, Janice clicked on her flashlight and headed back to her own tent. She almost screamed when she popped her head in and saw Nate lying there with Daisy on his chest.

"You scared the shit out of me," she whispered loudly.

"Who were you expecting?" he asked.

"I wasn't expecting anyone." Zipping the tent closed, she got into her sleeping bag and rubbed Daisy's ear affectionately. "How's she doing?"

"Still not one hundred percent, but she's getting there."

"What are you doing here?"

"Your father sent me to talk some sense into you."

Janice scowled at him. Of course. He couldn't have come here to see her and sneak in some kisses. No, he was doing her father's bidding. "I haven't made any decision yet, but when I do you can tell my father you did all you could." She flipped over and turned her back on him.

"He doesn't want you to be swindled."

"Charlie would be paying me from the grant the government has given him. I'm not paying a dime."

"You saw the grant paperwork?"

"He emailed it to me. I glanced at it briefly and spoke to his parole officer, but I didn't have time to give it the attention it deserves because I have a retreat going on."

Daisy climbed off him and on to her and licked her cheek before curling up in the corner of the tent. Nate spooned up next to her and put his arm around her. "I think it's a bad idea."

"You think everything is a bad idea," she said, shrugging him off.

"That's not true. I think you taking Donovan and Trent on this camping trip is a good idea."

"I'm so glad you approve," she said icily.

"Donovan said his father is a grifter. That he cheats people. Don't give him your bank account number. Make sure his check clears before you give him anything."

"Nate, if the check bounces, he goes back to jail. His parole officer was very convincing about that part of it. Why is it so hard for you to give someone a second chance?"

"His own son hates his guts. That should tell you something."

"It tells me that Donovan and his father's relationship is none of my business and has nothing to do with me. Besides, it's the holidays. Don't you think that this could be a Christmas miracle, getting them back together again?"

"Darlin', sometimes daddies are just toxic."

"Tell me about it," she muttered, fluffing up her camping pillow and wishing she was in her own bed instead.

"Frank isn't toxic. He's just set in his ways."

"Like someone else I know," she said, closing her eyes. Maybe if she pretended she was asleep, Nate would get the message and go home. He could leave Daisy here, though. She was warm and cuddly.

"You think I'm like your father?" he growled.

"There are similarities," she said, despite her decision to stop talking to him.

Nate sighed. "I'm not like Pete, am I?"

"Pete who?" She yawned.

"Doc Pete."

"No," she agreed. "You're nothing like him."

He was quiet for so long that Janice dozed off, but she startled awake when Nate rolled in close to her. The rasp of his five-o'clock shadow was erotic in the dark of the tent.

"Is that right?" He nibbled on her earlobe and she quaked from the sensation.

Nate put his arm around her again and unzipped her sleeping bag.

"What are you doing?" she asked as he pulled the material aside.

He cupped her breast and squeezed gently, rubbing his thumb over her nipple. "I'm showing you how much of a good idea I think camping is."

She muffled a snort of laughter and leaned into his caress. Janice wasn't quite ready to forgive him for being her father's lackey on the whole Charlie Lincoln proposition, but Nate was on the right track to getting back in her good graces. "I'm pretty sure my father didn't send you out to seduce me."

"What Frank doesn't know won't hurt him."

Damn straight. Janice wiggled closer to him and arched her neck to give his mouth better access.

"Mmmm," she hummed as he reached down and unbuttoned her pants. "I'm not sure what you think we're going to get away with out here, but I don't want to be embarrassed tomorrow."

"Then, keep it down," he said, unzipping her zipper. When he slid his hand into her panties, she spread her legs to give him access.

"Nate," she whispered as his magical fingers went to work between her thighs. She could feel his hardness pressing against her backside, even through two sets of clothes and her sleeping bag. Janice had to bite her lip to keep from groaning as his fingers flickered inside her.

Unable to take it a minute longer, she rolled to face him. Pressing her mouth against his in a hot, desperate kiss, she fumbled with his belt buckle. She was determined to drive him as crazy as he was driving her. Their tongues met and she thrust her hand into his pants. Nate moaned low into her mouth when she took a hold of his hard cock and began to pump him in the same rhythm he was using in between her legs. Frantic, she kissed him harder. Riding his fingers, she trembled on the edge of orgasm. Just as she was about to explode, he took his hand away. About to protest, she shucked off her clothes when she saw him do the same thing. It was tight quarters inside the two-man tent, but they managed not to roll over on the dog or knock over the tent poles that were securing it to the ground.

Kneeling up next to him, she ran her hands over every inch of him. She loved his hard muscles and the sexy stallion tattoos on his arms.

"You're so beautiful," he whispered, dipping his head to take her nipple in his mouth.

Her head lolled back on her neck, and Janice held him there. Straddling his knee, she rocked herself on it, needing the friction to bring her back toward the orgasm that had just been in reach.

"You want something?" he said, coming up for air.

"You," she whispered. "Always you."

"Always?" he said, putting on a condom.

Nodding, she lay back, wincing as she hit a rock. Shifting a bit, she tried to rein in her excitement. She didn't want to lose control and have the whole camp talking about this tomorrow over eggs and coffee.

But then he slipped inside her and her toes curled in pleasure. His heavy weight nearly took her breath away, pinning her to the ground. Then he thrust deep, and she couldn't even think about anything except the exquisite feel of him moving in and out of her. Nate made slow love to her and she clenched around him as the elusive orgasm she had been chasing crested. She opened her mouth and screamed silently.

So damned good.

He grunted in approval, but never sped up. It was bliss. Janice sighed and arched into his every stroke. She languidly stroked the back of his neck, enjoying his harsh breaths in her ear.

"Please," she whimpered, needing him to go faster, harder, deeper.

He chuckled. "I like hearing you beg."

"Nate." Janice kissed him, feeling his entire body tense and tremble. "Harder," she whispered.

He choked out a curse and pulled her tight against him. Kneeling up, he pressed the backs of her legs straight up. She almost kicked the tent over when he plunged deep and hard into her. The fast slaps of his body against hers sounded loud in the night, but she wouldn't stop him for anything.

"More," she begged and he complied. Janice came hard, pulling the sleeping bag over her face, she used it to muffle her scream of pleasure.

His groan as his release swamped over him, however, reverberated out and she panicked a bit even as she wanted to hear more. Panting, they froze where they were and listened frantically. Janice didn't hear any giggles or anyone angrily telling them to get a room. It was possible that anyone who wasn't sleeping was engaging in the same activity. Diego and Tracie, and Sam and Heidi most definitely. She didn't want to think about what her sisters were up to.

She and Nate cleaned up with some wipes and stuffed the trash into a bag.

"Stick around, cowboy," she said, wincing at the crick in her back.

"Not on your life. I've got to get up in a few hours." He gave a soft whistle to Daisy, who yawned and stretched.

"Take me with you," she said, as he pulled his clothes back on.

"I'll see you tomorrow. Think about what I said about Donovan's dad."

She tossed a pillow at him. "Butt out."

"Fine." He had the nerve to roll his eyes at her, but at least he took the trash with him.

Unfortunately, Daisy trotted out of the tent after her master and Janice was left all alone.

"Jerk," she said aloud in the darkness, hoping he heard her.

Chapter Sixteen

NATE DUG HIS hands in the pockets of his jacket and concentrated on not scowling at the Boy Scouts dressed as elves tossing candy canes out to the crowd. He hadn't been able to weasel out of Frank's plan to escort Janice and her retreat group to the Christmas parade. And he hadn't been able to talk her out of going through with Charlie Lincoln's ex-con retreats. At least she was doing her due diligence and Donovan had volunteered to work on as a guard. He assured Nate and Frank that he'd be able to keep his old man on the straight and narrow, even if he had to shoot him to do it. Frank had laughed, but Nate thought Donovan had been serious.

Everyone at the parade was having a great time. Everyone except him. Nate just wanted to go home. Doc Pete, Janice and Seth Honeyman were laughing and talking together like it was a veterinarian party. Janice belonged with a man like Pete. Not with a man like him, who couldn't imagine the inconvenience of blocking off Main Street for the weekend while tourists flooded the street looking for bargains. He bet that when Doc Pete romanced a girl, it wasn't in a cheap two-man tent in his backyard. Doc Pete probably had a personal chef on call who could whip up steak and lobster on a moment's notice. He probably also had a bedroom that looked like a palace and didn't share it with a bed-hogging Australian shepherd.

Looking around, he saw Diego and Tracie stuffing their faces with cookies and Sam and Heidi kissing under every piece of mistletoe they could find. Trent was driving the float that had some of his students on mechanical bulls.

That was a lawsuit waiting to happen, Nate thought grimly, refusing to wave back as the kids waved their hats in the air and whooped it up for the crowd. Kelly and Alissa were riding their horses behind the float. Their horses' manes had been decorated with red and green ribbons and jingle bells. They made a racket.

All the Christmas cheer made him itch and Nate decided that he'd wait until after the weekend to drop off the toys for the toy drive that the fire department was running. The ranch hands had all chipped in and Esteban had bought a truckload of toys. He was about to make his getaway and sneak down Wisteria Lane now that the parade had passed, when he saw one of Janice's retreat guests, the bartender with the purple hair, struggling to pull away from an angry-looking fella.

Nate could use a bit of blowing off steam, so he strode up to them and caught the last part of the argument.

"You need to come home now, Regina. This bullshit has gone on long enough."

"I have one more week. You promised, Ernie."

"It's bad enough I have to deal with your late hours

when you're bartending. Now you fuck off for two weeks with your girlfriends. I think you're cheating on me."

Nate paused, not wanting to give credence to the man's suspicions by butting in. But then he started dragging her off toward the parking lot and Regina was pulling back.

"Highwater!" Nate bellowed, flagging down Shane Highwater, Last Stand's police chief.

Shane looked over and followed Nate's finger to Regina and Ernie. Regina was struggling now in earnest. Eyes narrowed, Shane headed over. Nate was closer, so he intercepted.

"Let her go, asshat. She doesn't want to go with you."

"Who the hell are you?"

"I'm the guy stopping you from being arrested." He jerked his thumb at Highwater who was bearing down on them at a fast clip.

Ernie let go of Regina, who backed away rubbing her arm. "I said I'll be home next week."

"You're coming home tonight," Ernie said, advancing again on Regina—but Nate stepped in front of her.

Only he wasn't expecting Ernie to sucker punch him in the gut. He doubled over. Highwater was on Ernie in a heartbeat, two hundred pounds of pissed-off police chief. Nate almost felt sorry for the guy. Highwater had him handcuffed and subdued faster than Nate could take down a runaway calf.

"Are you all right?" Regina said. "He didn't mean it."

Wincing, Nate straightened up and rubbed his stomach. He almost wished Highwater wasn't so efficient because he'd have liked to have gone a few rounds with Ernie. "He meant it all right."

"Are you pressing charges?" Highwater asked.

"You're damned right I am."

"You can't," Regina said and tugged him away from Ernie and Highwater.

"Why not?"

"Because he'll take it out on me," she said simply.

"Not if he's dead," Nate growled and advanced on Ernie.

Regina tugged him back and Rita, Janice and the other women from the retreat were suddenly there.

"What's going on?" Janice asked, stepping between him and Ernie.

"This asshole punched me in the gut. Regina doesn't want me to press charges because he'll take it out on her," Nate said loudly, making sure Highwater heard him.

Regina burst into tears. Ernie started swearing and Janice said, "What did you do to make him punch you?"

Really? "Not a damned thing."

"He's sleeping with my wife," Ernie shouted, trying to pull out of the death grip Highwater had him in.

"I don't even know who your wife is," Nate said.

Janice pointed at Regina.

"Oh," he said. "No, I'm sleeping with her." He pointed to Janice.

"What?" a new voice said, sounding both shocked and amused.

Oh no.

"Mom," Janice said, mortification flooding her tone.

"I suppose I shouldn't have said that." He hadn't noticed Sarah coming up—with Doc Pete no less. Maybe he should attack Ernie back and spend the next few days in a jail cell, because he was in hot water.

"Damn it, Nate," Janice growled.

Highwater shook his head and said, "Well, I don't care who is sleeping with whom. I'm a witness to the assault. I saw this jackass hit you without provocation. He needs to calm down some anyway, so I'm going to take him down and process him."

"I want my lawyer," Ernie said.

"Good," Highwater replied, hauling him toward his squad car. "That'll take me most of the day."

Nate inched toward them, but Janice shoved him back with both hands. "You have all the sense of a bull. How could you?" She turned back to comfort Regina and the retreat group.

Pete looked embarrassed and excused himself. Sarah gave him a stern glance before following Pete.

Crap. What if he had just ruined things between Pete and Janice? Nate tamped down the feeling of satisfaction. That wasn't fair to anyone. Fuck a duck. What if Sarah told Frank?

THE PARADE HAD been a total shit show with Regina's soon-to-be ex showing up and Nate blabbing to everyone that they were lovers. But some retail therapy at the Christmas booths, after Rita got Regina centered, had put the retreat back into a festive mood. Janice avoided her mother, but Sarah hadn't said anything about Nate's announcement at the tree-lighting ceremony. It helped that Nate had made himself scarce.

After the tree lighting, it was tradition to go back to the ranch and find out who your secret Santa was this year. Janice was tickled that her retreat was going to be a part of it. They would all exchange gifts on their last day, after the cattle drive.

Her father also invited Pete to take part and she was surprised when he agreed. But he had done so much for them his year, he was almost like family. He was chatting with Rita over hors d'oeuvres that her mom had set up by the punch-bowl. Janice hoped that he would buy Rita a few cows so Frank would get off Janice's back about what that meant. It meant he knew how to buy a cow as an investment.

At least that's what she hoped it meant. As far as she was concerned, anyone with eyes could see that Rita was interested in him. Janice only hoped Pete could sense that, too. And after Nate had staked his claim in the middle of Main Street this morning, Pete would have to be deaf not to have heard Janice was spoken for.

While it was hard not to play matchmaker and team up Tracie and Heidi with their beaus, it was more fun when everyone tried to guess who their Santa was. She hoped she didn't get Nate or her family because she had already picked out their gifts. Reaching into the big empty chili pot, she pulled out a slip of paper. Keeping her face neutral, she read

Gayle's name. Pleased that she'd got someone from the retreat, she stuffed it in her pocket and walked over to the punchbowl where she could watch everyone's faces and see if they gave away any clues.

Nate walked over to the chili pot. He was swaying slightly on his feet. She was pretty sure he'd been drinking his way through the Christmas market, sampling a beer here, a glass of wine there. While she was happy that he was starting to relax, she didn't think he was completely there yet.

She flicked her eyes to her father, but he was laughing with Suze and stuffing his mouth with her cream puffs. If Sarah had told him about Nate, he was hiding it well.

Craning her neck, Janice tried to see whose name was on the piece of paper Nate picked out. But after he squinted at it, Nate jammed it into the pocket of his Levi's. As she picked her way over to him, he stepped outside.

"Janice," her father called. He was talking with Pete and waving her over.

"One minute, Dad." Janice darted outside and saw that Nate was heading back to his cottage.

"Wait up," she said, jogging out to meet him.

He reluctantly halted and tapped his foot impatiently as she came closer. "If you came out here to holler at me, I don't want to hear it."

"No hollering, I promise. What's done is done. Although, as far as I can tell no one has mentioned your crass announcement to my father...yet."

Sighing, Nate crossed his arms over his chest. "I'm sorry about that. I wasn't thinking."

"Where are you going?" She held up her punch cup. "There's still eggnog left."

"I've had enough Christmas for one day. I've got to go check on Daisy."

Alarm pierced through her. "I thought she was doing all right. Is she keeping her food down?"

Nate held up his hands and she stopped moving toward him. "No, she's fine. I'm just worried about her."

"Oh," Janice said, rocking back on her heels. "Who did you get for secret Santa?"

A ghost of a smile passed briefly over his face. "That's cheating."

She looked over her shoulder to see if anyone had followed her out. "I won't tell anyone."

He shook his head. "Oh no, you don't. You're going to have to wait until after the cattle drive next week, just like everyone else."

Stepping in close, she danced her fingers up his shirt. "I bet I can make you talk."

"Is that right?"

Her entire body shivered when he closed the distance between them and dipped his head.

"Janice!" Frank hollered from the porch.

"Damn it," she said, glaring back at her father. "We'll continue this later." But when she turned back to Nate he had already walked away. She stomped back to the ranch house porch. "What? What is so important?"

"You're neglecting our guests," he said and jerked his head to the party.

"No, I'm not." Everyone was having a great time without her there to act like a mother hen. The retreat gals would go back to the retreat center or the bunkhouse, depending on if some hanky-panky was going on. And for their sakes, she hoped there was. This was their getaway and their vacation. It was none of her business where they slept.

"Leave Nate alone," Frank said.

So that was what this was about. Janice set her jaw and crossed her arms. "Nate and I are adults and it's none of your business what he does when he's not working."

"He's not the man for you."

"I've got news for you, Dad. Yes, he is. He has been since we were both sixteen. And now that we're consenting adults, it's none of your business."

"You are my daughter and it is my business. I don't want to see you hurt."

"How can you say that?" she said. "Nate would never hurt me. We're friends. We always have been."

"I think he's a great friend. But that's not what we're talking about here."

She didn't want to have this conversation with her father right now. She wanted to have a nice peaceful holiday. The stress from the near bankruptcy and the thousand things that had gone wrong as they tried to keep the ranch out of the red this year had taken its toll on all of them.

"I think you need to go inside and have some eggnog and butt out of my life." To her horror, she felt tears glisten at the corners of her eyes. Oh no. Oh *hell* no. Not now. Not in front of her father. He never believed they were tears of anger. She turned her back on him before he could see them. Janice was going to have to tell Nate that the jig was up. Frank knew and was being reasonable about it. It was always worse when he didn't yell. It was easy to ignore him when he yelled.

"I want you to marry Pete Dickerson."

She had to have heard that wrong. Whipping back around, she said, "What did you say?"

Frank held up placating hands to her. "Hear me out. I think you're a good match. He's looking to put down roots. You have a lot in common and he'd be good to you."

"He's also rich," she said sarcastically. "I'm sure that fact hasn't slipped your mind. What does Pete think about your matchmaking?"

"I haven't brought it up to him."

That was something at least.

"Yet."

"Don't you dare," she warned. "This isn't the Middle Ages. You don't get to marry off a daughter for profit."

"It's not me who's profiting from this."

She raised an eyebrow.

"Not entirely."

"Dad, Pete's a great guy. I admire and respect him."

"That's a great foundation for a marriage."

"But I don't love him. I love…" She cut herself off. She was not going to tell her father she loved Nate before she got the chance to say it to the man himself.

"What's love got to do with it?"

"I hope you're singing Tina Turner songs because otherwise I can't believe you just said that."

"You and Pete suit. You and Nate don't. He's too much like me. I love him like a son, but he won't make you happy."

"He does make me happy." When he wasn't being a pig-headed, stubborn ass. Which, now that she thought about it, had been a lot lately.

"You are too different. He will run roughshod all over your feelings. I know because that's what I do."

"That's what you're doing." Janice felt herself softening toward her father, though. "I know you mean well, and that you have my best interests at heart. But I need to choose who I marry, not you."

"Janice," her father said, looking as defeated as she had ever seen him. "If you don't marry Pete, I'm afraid we're going to lose the ranch."

Panic thundered through her. "Why? What aren't you telling me?" She thought back to the finances and her conversations with Emily and Kelly. They weren't in great shape, but in the time she and her sisters had been back, there had been an improvement. With Trent's bull-riding school bringing in more students who wanted portraits, Kelly was doing very well. Emily's wind turbines were being built and once they were up, the ranch wouldn't have to worry so much about bills. And with Rita and Charlie's retreats, she was finally pulling her weight as well.

"Emily thinks beef cattle is a losing business."

Janice frowned trying to connect the dots. "How is me marrying for money going to change that?"

"It'll mean she can build her dairy and me and Nate can still sell cattle."

"Wait, slow down. Emily isn't planning on shutting down the cattle business."

"Isn't she?"

Emily had been pretty vocal about her opinion on slaughtering cattle for food. But quite frankly, Janice had just tuned her out. She loved her sister, but they didn't see eye to eye. Especially not on the subject of bacon and steak. However, the changes her father was talking about weren't something that could happen overnight. And certainly not when their finances were in a flux. Janice couldn't risk defaulting on her loans and losing her horses. "She's not in charge yet," Janice said. "And that's way in the future. A lot can happen in between now and then."

"Don't think I don't know you'll side with her when it comes out. You both think it's inhumane."

"The ranch hands could treat the cattle better, and you could look at them as sentient creatures instead of a line on a ledger."

"See," he said.

Janice still wasn't sure what that had to do with Pete. "So if I marry Pete, you'll finally listen to me about resting the cows?"

"If you marry Pete, I'll retire tomorrow and Emily can have her dairy farm as long as Nate and I keep our herds of cattle."

"That's not retiring, Dad."

He shook his head. "What do you care?"

"I care that you're killing yourself and Nate trying to make the cattle profitable. If you retire, I think the cattle could be more of a hobby than a business."

"A hobby," he sputtered.

Whoa! She did not want to go down that road. She tried to steer the conversation back to what was important. "Besides, I don't love Pete and he doesn't love me. I think he would be offended if I wanted to marry him for his money. That never works out well. You wouldn't want one of us to marry a gold digger, would you?"

"You're not a gold digger. You and your sisters will inherit this ranch, provided I can keep us in the black. I'm trying the best way I know how."

"What's going on out here?" Kelly said. She and Emily had come out to investigate.

"Dad wants me to marry Pete for his money."

"What?" Emily said, laughing.

"Not just his money," Frank said. "They'd make good couple. They like the same things. They have a lot in common. They have the same temperament."

"Sounds like they'd be better off as friends," Emily said.

"Not to mention, Janice has someone else in mind to marry," Kelly teased.

Oh, great. Janice shook her head at Kelly, but her father caught the gesture.

"Who?" Frank's eyes narrowed.

"Dad is worried that we are going to lose the Three Sisters Ranch," Janice added, changing the subject.

"What?" Emily cried. "Not a chance."

Kelly crossed her arms over her chest. "We'll be all right. We just need to hang tight."

Frank's fist clenched. "We need the money. All I'm saying is that marriages have gotten started on a lot less than mutual respect and friendship."

Emily made a face. "Aw, Dad, that's so romantic…not. Look, we've got it covered. You sent for us. We came. We're going to be all right. You don't have to sell Janice to the highest bidder like she's a prize heifer."

"Thank you so much for that comparison," Janice said, putting her hands on her hips.

"She's right," Kelly said. "My portrait studio is making a profit—profit I can invest in the ranch. Janice's retreat center has two long-term contracts."

"Yeah," her father said. "One that's going to bring hardened criminals to our doorstep. Aren't you worried about your daughter?"

"My daughter won't be near the retreat center while their group is there and she's never alone. If her father and I aren't with her, you and Mom or her aunts are. Alissa will be fine. I think it's a kind program and something that would be very useful not only for the prisoners, but also for society."

Janice was thrilled to have Kelly's support. She had been worried about what Trent and Kelly would think, and if they were worried about Alissa.

"If it's on the up and up," Frank growled.

"Donovan is seeing to that," Emily said. "And trust me, no one wants to catch Charlie Lincoln pulling a scam more than Donovan does. If he is not one hundred percent legitimate, we'll know immediately."

"And the deal will be off," Janice assured her father.

"I just don't want you girls to be hurt. I just want to keep you safe."

They each hugged him.

"Dad, we've got this. Let us take care of you and Mom for a change," Emily said.

"Or at least, trust us to help out by managing our businesses to assist the ranch," Kelly said.

"It doesn't work like that," Frank grumbled. "I'm your father and it's my job to take care of you. I might not be the best father, but I do my best."

"We know you do," Janice said. "It's going to be all right. Let's go back inside before people start looking for us." Kelly and Emily each took him by the arm and walked him back to the party.

Janice looked over her shoulder toward Nate's cottage. She wanted to go to him, but she was sick of being pushed away. She didn't want to think her father was right about them not being a good match, but it seemed every step they took toward being a couple, he retreated the next day as if he regretted it.

And the last thing she wanted was to be someone's regret.

Chapter Seventeen

JANICE HAD THE retreat up at four a.m. again. There were fewer grumbles and more of a gritty excitement in the air. They headed over to the bunkhouse and grabbed plates. Janice helped herself to a stack of pancakes and some sausages and sat across the table from Nate.

"Are you sure you want to come with us?" she asked.

"Are you afraid I'll see something that will bench your group?" he countered.

She shook her head. "It's just I'm surprised you're letting Esteban take the lead today."

Nate drunk his coffee. "It's just one day. And I need to make sure your group isn't going to be a liability."

"What are you going to have us do?"

"We're going to head on over to Asteroid pasture and spread out some hay. Then we'll check the fencing. Repair it, if it needs it. Check the pond. And that will be before lunch."

Ugh. Janice didn't let her reaction to the tough schedule show on her face. "We can handle that."

"I'll be the judge of that."

"You're an asshole in the morning," she told him cheerfully.

"I'm always an asshole," he said.

True. But she loved the idiot anyway. "Can we talk about the other night?"

They hadn't had a moment together since the Christmas-tree lighting and even though she was just as busy as he was, she wanted to make sure they were all right. That nothing had changed.

"Not now," he said, getting up from the table.

"Later," she demanded. "After dinner. I'll bring dessert."

He gave her a long smoldering look that curled her toes and made her think that maybe she would be dessert. Nate nodded slowly and she felt every nerve ending in her body come to life.

Yeah, they were still good.

Janice rode in the back, fretting over Tracie and Regina. They were doing better in the saddle, but they were still bouncing around. They were going to be sore as hell. Maybe she could afford to put in an outdoor hot tub after a few retreats to help soothe any tired and battered muscles.

Nate worked them hard all morning, shouting orders and generally doing his best to be surly and unpleasant.

"Don't let him get to you," she said to her group. "He's all bark and no bite."

They were finishing up the fencing when Rita and Sarah drove up in a mini chuck wagon, the actual one having to be used for the main group. Janice didn't care. She was happy to help carry the picnic table out of the bed of the truck and set up the umbrella over it so they could all eat in the shade.

It was a simple lunch. Hot dogs and burgers on the portable charcoal grill. Her mother's world-famous potato salad and buttered corn on the cob rounded out the meal. And not one of the peanut butter cookies was left by the time Nate sat down to eat. It served him right. But she had saved him his favorite, which was chocolate chip anyway. They must have drunk their weight in sweet tea and lemonade and Janice was thankful that there was a porta potty set up outside of the pasture.

"How did we do?" Janice asked Nate as they rode back to the ranch after finishing up the fences. It was early by ranching time, so Nate was proving that he was a big softie by letting them out hours before a normal day would end.

"Keep Regina and Tracie in the back of the herd. Gayle is your strongest rider. I'll pair her up with Chaz. Suze ropes pretty well from what I've seen, so I'll put her with Esteban. The other two can ride on the sides. Just make sure—"

"They don't get in the middle of the herd," Janice finished.

"Exactly."

She squeezed his leg. "Thank you."

"No thanks necessary. You did a bang-up job getting them ready and those crazy bitches are enjoying it." He shook his head. "I can't wrap my brain around it."

"You enjoy it, too."

"Yeah, but you're paying me to do this. Not the other way around."

Janice looked back at her group. They were dusty and tired, but they were grinning from ear to ear. "It's good to work hard. To make a difference. This is not only a type of therapy for them, it's a vacation."

"No. A vacation is lying on a beach in Hawaii drinking a mai tai and inspecting bikinis. This is work."

"Bikini inspector, huh?" Janice wrinkled her nose at him.

"Now that's a job you wouldn't have to pay me to do."

She slugged him in the arm. "You're a pig."

"You got a bikini?" Nate asked, unfazed.

"I skinny-dip."

"You do not," he said.

"I could start."

"I wouldn't recommend it."

"Why not?"

"Leeches."

"There are no leeches in the pond."

"You sure about that?"

"I was. I'm not anymore." Janice scowled at him. "I'm going to stick with the pool at the Y."

"I wouldn't go skinny-dipping then. They'll kick you out for that."

"Thanks for the advice," she said dryly.

As they rode up to the ranch, Nate asked her to take care of his horse for him. He wanted to check on Jonas before dinner. After they got the horses brushed, fed and watered, the women went back to the retreat center to shower. Janice was looking forward to a long hot shower herself and hoped that no one had the same idea back at the ranch house. However, as she approached, the cacophony of barking dogs made her pick up her pace.

She recognized Regina's ex-husband Ernie. He was pounding on her parents' front door. Fingers trembling, Janice pulled out her cell phone and called the police. Sheriff Highwater said he'd send over Officer Velasquez right away. Then she called her mother.

"Hello, dear."

"Where are you?"

"Rita and I are at the bunkhouse getting ready for dinner, why?"

"Where is Dad?"

"He decided to go micromanage Esteban. What's all that noise?"

"Ernie, the jerk from the parade, is banging on the front door. The dogs are going nuts and I called the police. Where's Alissa?"

"She's at the riding school with her parents. Where's Nate? You need to avoid this Ernie character until the police get here."

Of course, at that moment Ernie turned around to stalk back to his car and saw her.

"Too late." Janice hung up with her mother and looked at him. "You need to leave this ranch right now. You are not welcome here." How did he even get past the gate? "The police are on their way."

"Where's my wife?" Ernie stalked over to her.

A shot of fear went down her spine. She did not want this confrontation. "That's none of your business. You've got to go."

"Make me."

"You put a hand on me and I'll make sure you rot in prison for a long time."

"My lawyer will bond me out in an hour, but you'll be picking your teeth off the ground."

Janice tried to remember her self-defense, but decided to run instead. She pretended to throw something at him and when he ducked, she whirled and ran for the barn. If she could make it there in time and close the door before he got to it, she could wait him out until the police got here. But she was tired and aching from putting in a hard day's work in the saddle and she was too slow. Ernie was closing in on her.

The rifle shot startled them both. Janice stumbled, but recovered first and kept running.

"Don't fucking move," Donovan said, racking in another round. He had fired in the air. "You take another step and I will put you in the ground."

Nate and Emily were rapidly approaching from the other direction on the Gator.

"You wouldn't dare," Ernie said.

"I put down feral hogs all the time. What's one more?"

"Donovan," Janice said shakily. "Don't kill him."

"That's up to him." Donovan's eyes were stone cold and Janice was a little afraid of him. "Your mom called me all upset. Luckily, I was out back in her garden waiting for some deer to come by for a snack."

"Does Emily know this?" Janice said as the Gator roared up to them.

"She will now," he sighed resignedly.

"I got this Donovan," Nate said, climbing out.

"You've got what?" Janice shrieked as Nate full-on tackled Ernie to the ground.

He pounded his fist into Ernie's face as Ernie tried to cover up. "Not so tough now, you son of a bitch, are you?"

"Nate that's enough," Janice said. "You're going to get in trouble."

"It's self-defense," Nate said, continuing to pummel Ernie.

Ernie miraculously kicked out from under Nate and got on top. He drove several punches into Nate's body.

"Let me see that." Janice held out her hand for Donovan's rifle.

"No," he said.

"Fine." Janice ran up to the porch and opened up the door. Seven dogs came thundering out and piled on to Ernie, snarling and nipping. Springing up, Ernie scuttled away from the dogs. Janice whistled and they came back to her side.

Nate quickly got up, shaking his head to clear it. He kept his fists up and waited. Ernie wiped his bloody nose with his sleeve. A police siren wailed faintly in the distance.

"You're going to jail for assault," Ernie said.

"You're coming with me." Nate grinned. "Better hope they don't put us in the same cell."

"You entered this properly illegally. The gate was closed and somehow you circumvented it," Janice cried. "Nate was only protecting me."

"The gate was open and he attacked me without provocation." Ernie pointed at Nate.

"You a lawyer now?" Donovan said.

"I know my rights," Ernie countered. "And you threat-ened to kill me. Shot at me. That's attempted murder."

"If I wanted to murder you, you'd already be dead and I'd drag you back to a feral hog nest. There's be nothing left of you."

"On that note," Emily said, glaring at her fiancé. "We have security cameras that recorded everything."

We do? Janice frowned at her sister, not sure if she was bluffing or not.

"Cameras?" Ernie said, looking around for them.

"Don't bother. You won't see them. What's the point in having them, if every moron off the street could avoid them? I've sent the entire footage to Chief Highwater's office." Emily jiggled her phone at him.

"You little bitch."

"Give me an excuse," Donovan said. "Please."

"Don't bother with him, Donovan. He violated Regina's restraining order when he came here." Janice folded her arms around herself, trying to stop herself from bursting into tears. She was so damned angry, she wanted to tear Ernie apart. "He's in enough legal trouble to keep him out of our hair and Regina's for a long time."

Ernie seethed and a muscle worked in his jaw. Janice could tell he wanted to say something. To do something, but with Nate and Donovan there, he was too much of a coward to attack her.

What if Alissa and Sarah had been in the house? Would

he have threatened a little girl and her grandmother? It was her retreat that brought him here. Was she putting her family at risk? And now, Nate and Donovan might get in trouble for protecting her.

A Last Stand police car drove up to them and Officer Velasquez got out. After taking all their statements and confirming that Ernie had violated the restraining order, Ernie got his second ride handcuffed in the back of a police car.

"What do you think is going to happen now?" Janice asked.

Nate came up to her. "You need to shut the retreat down. It's too dangerous. Can you imagine what the next retreat will be like with Charlie's ex-cons? Start up a dressage school instead. Forget about these retreats. The people are damaged and are putting you at risk. I can't have that."

"Nate." She put her hand on his arm. This was hard because a small part of her agreed with him. Not the damaged people part, but the danger. Tears flowed down her cheek and she ignored them. Maybe if she ignored them, everyone else would too.

Unfortunately, Nate wasn't wired like that and he pulled her into his arms for a giant hug that would have felt great if she wasn't ready to rip someone's head off. Wiggling free, she said, "There's always going to be some dickhead who wants to throw his weight around. My retreats are important. I'm not canceling this one. Along with Rita's therapy sessions, it's given Regina the courage to finally start divorce proceedings."

"So that's why he's so mad? A fat lot of good that restraining order did when he was threatening you. A piece of paper isn't going to keep you safe."

"It's going to make it difficult for him to do it again."

"You know what will stop him? If you kick the retreat out. Let them go to Jameson or to Rita's office for their therapy."

"That's not the only reason why they're here. They're here for the animals, for nature, and yeah, to play cowgirl for a day."

"I don't care about them," Nate said. "I care about you. You are not safe here, giving these types of retreats."

"I am safe. I had Donovan and you and my dogs. Yours too." She pointed down at Daisy, who was wagging her tail happily.

"You could have been hurt. You could have gotten the dogs hurt. This was irresponsible."

Janice reacted like he had slapped her. That was a low blow. "What?" How could he say that to her? If anyone was being irresponsible, it would have been Donovan threatening to shoot Ernie. Not that she didn't understand the feeling. Ernie could use a good shooting.

"We need to go do something," Emily said, dragging Donovan by the arm back to the Gator.

"What?" Donovan asked.

"Something that isn't anywhere near this argument."

"We're not arguing," Nate said.

"He's right," Janice said. "There's nothing to argue about because I'm not stopping my retreats. Any of them. And there's not a damn thing Nate can do about it." She crossed her arms over her chest and glared at him.

"Shut it down, Janice. It's not worth the money."

"It is. It's worth more than the money. People are counting on me." Janice gave a disgusted wave to Emily as she and Donovan took off on the Gator. "I'm not going to disappoint those women who have worked their butts off for over a week."

"Then I am. They're not going on the cattle drive."

Shock stole her breath and she could only gape at him. This wasn't Nate. This was something her father would do. "You can't do that."

"I can and I will. Send the boohoo club home."

"You promised."

"You promised," he said, "that I had full control. That if I didn't think they were ready they would be benched."

"They worked their asses off today." Janice was yelling and she didn't care if it made her sound hysterical or not.

Nate looked away, probably because he knew she was right.

"Don't do this," she begged.

"Your tears aren't going to work on me."

"My tears are the only thing that's stopping me from punching your lights out."

Nate shook his head. "What are we doing, Janice? This isn't us."

"I know it's not." She hugged herself, trying not to sob. She hated this. She wished she wasn't crying. It made her look weak or like she was looking for sympathy and she wasn't. She was so pissed off, she couldn't see straight. "You're not like this. You know I'm right. You're reacting because you're scared." Janice hiccupped. "And I can understand that." She fought to keep her voice even and steady, even though she was ready to shake apart. "But you need to trust me."

"I do trust you." His voice softened. "But you're too sweet to see that there are types of men in this world who will use you and wring you dry. Charlie Lincoln is one of them. Ernie is another."

"Ernie has no power over me."

"In a perfect world, that would be true. But the reality is that son of a bitch is probably going to press charges against the ranch for assault and for threatening him with a deadly weapon."

"That's on you," she argued. "And Donovan."

"Yes, but we did it because you were in danger. What would have happened if we hadn't come along?"

Janice took a deep breath. She didn't want to think about it.

"What happens next time?"

"There won't be a next time," she said.

"Yeah, there will. There always is. Trust me. I've lived this. The ranch has had a good run, but our luck was bound to run out. I won't stand by and watch you get hurt. You have other dreams—not just this retreat center. Forget about the therapy groups and concentrate on the horses." He reached to put a hand on her shoulder, but she knocked it away.

"You can't stop us from joining the cattle drive on Friday."

"I can move it to Thursday or wait until Sunday, when they're gone."

"You'd let the cattle suffer for a few days just to win an argument?" She shook her head. "Maybe Emily is right. You'd never let a milk cow go without milking for a day or two. But since these cows are set to be slaughtered next year, who cares?" Janice knew she was being unfair, but she couldn't stop the words coming out of her mouth. She wanted to shake him out of the cold, surly mood he had been in the past few days. She wanted her Nate back.

"I hate it when Frank is right," he said, slumping. He rubbed his hand over his face.

"Me too," she said, bitterly. "Is there anything I can do to change your mind? Don't ruin Christmas for these women."

His head snapped up and his eyes were no longer cold. She stepped back from the raw pain and anger in them. "Christmas is one day and I'm so thankful for that. Life is full of disappointments. They'll get used to it. You'll get used to it."

"What happened to you?" she asked. "You used to love Christmas."

"I loved…" Nate cut off and closed his eyes. "I loved being with you. The rest of the bullshit could go hang."

Janice reached for his hand, but he stepped back.

"Don't," he said. "I'm exhausted. I'm at the end of my rope and I don't know why."

"It's because you've been working too hard. You need a vacation. You need some work-life balance."

He snorted. "Yeah, that's what I need all right." Nate gave a humorless laugh. "I got Doc Pete in the secret Santa."

Janice blinked at the sudden change in conversation. "What does that have to do with anything?"

"What do you think I should get the good doctor? What do you give the man who has everything?"

Janice floundered for a bit. How they got here, she hadn't a clue. She wanted to talk about how Nate had been burning the candle at both ends for too long. She wanted Nate to change his mind about the cattle drive. "I don't know. Get him a buck knife. Or a watch. He's constantly breaking his."

Nate snorted. "Maybe the man who has everything needs a woman who has everything."

"Oh no, you don't. I see what you're doing here. And I'll tell you what I told my father. I am not marrying Pete. I am not a prize to be won. I'm not a gift to be given. I like Pete, but I'm not going to marry him for his money. What type of friend does that?" She took in a deep, hurtful breath. "What kind of a lover gives up his mate so easily?"

"Easy?" He rubbed his forehead as if it was giving him great pain. "This isn't easy."

"Don't you dare walk away from me," Janice said, as he turned away.

Nate continued to walk back toward his cottage.

"Again."

Chapter Eighteen

NATE SHOULD HAVE known that Janice wouldn't go out without a fight. She had the boohoo club up and ready to go at four thirty a.m. every morning for the rest of the week. They followed the team out and worked as if they were a part of the group. Kelly and Emily joined in on Wednesday and Donovan joined them today. Nate was beginning to feel outnumbered.

And if looks could kill, he'd have been eviscerated by the glare those ladies gave him. They worked hard on the fences and hauling hay and feed. He couldn't, in good conscience, say that any one of them didn't pull their own weight.

He felt like an asshole too, but that wasn't anything new. He couldn't possibly feel any worse about himself than he did at this moment. He was going to lose his job once Emily decided to turn the ranch into a dairy farm. Or he was going to lose Janice—if his attitude hadn't already pushed her away—if she decided that Pete was a better choice, money or not. The only bright spots were Daisy and Jonas. Daisy had made a complete recovery and was back to hogging most of the bed. And while Jonas wasn't quite ready for work yet, he was going to be fine, too.

Nate supposed those were the only Christmas miracles he could hope for.

Worrying was keeping him from sleeping at night, but he drifted off on his horse and in the truck at lunchtime. He was more of a danger working cattle than the retreat was. At least when he was on Jonas, the horse knew what to do if Nate wasn't giving him commands. The new horse was still trying to figure out how much he could get away with.

Skipping dinner that night, Nate decided to drink himself to sleep. With the cattle drive being the next morning, it probably wasn't the brightest of ideas, but he needed to get some rest. Short of knocking himself out, he wasn't sure what else to do.

The booze must have worked because Nate was dreaming Donovan had finally lost his cool and took a machine gun to the feral hogs. Only, machine guns also didn't yell, "Open the damned door, Nate."

Squinting at the clock, he saw it was three a.m. He recognized the machine gun's voice. Who else could it be?

"Hold on to your ass," he growled and wobbled to a sitting position. Damn, his head was a throbbing mess and his mouth felt full of cotton. Maybe Janice had brought doughnuts or something. His stomach protested, but Nate ignored it and staggered to his feet. "Will you stop with the noise? I'm coming already." Damn.

He opened the door, and Janice pushed inside giving him a shoulder block that would make any hockey player proud. She was buzzing with purpose. If he believed in such nonsense, he would have been convinced she was some kind of vampire, sucking the energy from him and adding it to her own endless supply.

"I had a good half hour more," he complained.

"We're coming out with you today." Janice whirled on him. Now that he looked closer, she looked tired as well. This last week had been rough on her. Donovan had said that Frank was still trying to get her to reconsider the retreats altogether. Apparently, a dressage school was better than an ex-con retreat, which was saying something, considering how her father hated all that "fancy horse stuff."

"I kind of figured," he said. He should apologize. But then she might forgive him. And if she forgave him, he wouldn't be able to stop himself from dragging her back to bed. Of course, she'd probably tell him to go to hell, and he'd deserve it. But he really was sorry. He wasn't thinking straight lately. The headaches were getting worse and it made him snarly and snappish.

"If you have a problem with it, get it out now." Janice squared her shoulders and glared at him defiantly.

"Peace," he said, holding up a hand. "I need a bucket of coffee and some aspirin." More like a bucket of aspirin.

She wrinkled her nose. "What's wrong with you?"

"The list is long," he said and fumbled into the kitchen.

"Are you drunk?"

"No." Not anymore.

She moved as if to put a hand on his arm, but then stopped herself. That near broke his heart, but it was no more than he deserved. He'd tell her that the retreat did her proud. But not right now. Right now, it would be all he could do to get through this day.

"Pete's joining us today."

Nate had his back to her and closed his eyes. Of course he was. Why not? No doubt he'd be riding next to Janice and they'd be smiling and chatting.

"He's excited about the secret Santa tonight. I think he got Rita. What did you wind up getting him?"

Normally, he'd tease her and tell her she'd have to wait, but there didn't seem to be a point anymore. "I went with the buck knife."

"I got Gayle," she said. "I went with a gift certificate to Bella's Beauty Salon."

He wondered if the coffee really was taking an eternity or if it was just him. Nate wished he had the words to make everything seem less awkward, but he was using all his energy just to stand up. Maybe he should take a few days off. It they hadn't had so much damned work to do, he'd consider it. Last time he tried to take a few hours off, he decided to go hunting with Donovan and wound up falling asleep in the tree stand.

"My group has earned their place on the cattle drive. Do you promise you're not going to spoil this for them?"

"Yeah," he said. Finally, the coffee was brewing. He took a deep breath of the scent and then swapped out the pot for a cup and poured himself some, replacing the carafe when the cup was full. He blew on it and took a sip. It cut through some of the cobwebs. It was time to cowboy up and let her know how he felt.

"Janice, I'm sorry. You were right. I was afraid for you

and for what that asshole Ernie was going to do. Highwater called me and Donovan into his office and gave us hell, but that was the end of it. He personally drove Ernie out to the town limits and told him in no uncertain terms to fuck off. I was wrong to take it out on your retreat. They did a good job this week. You should be proud of them."

He waited, but she didn't say anything. Okay, he was still in the doghouse. "I'm not in a good place right now," he said. "My headaches are getting worse. I can hardly string two words together, and the ranch being on the brink of foreclosure is eating at me. Pete's a good man who would do right by you and your family. You may not love him now, but I don't think it's out of the question that you could love someone like him. I can't say I'd be happy about the match, though." He took a deep, shuddering breath and forced himself to say the next part, even though there were migraine flashers throbbing over his eyesight. "I figured, though, if you don't mind the hard work to keep this ranch afloat, and haven't come to your senses yet and realized that he's a much better man than I am, I'd like for you and I to make a go of this. I love you, Janice. I always have, and I've been an idiot."

He took a gulp of coffee, but as the silence grew, he began to sweat. His headache was almost unbearable. It was just a damned hangover, but it felt like someone was squeezing his head with a vise while jabbing an ice pick into his skull.

"Well, say something damn it." Nate whirled around.

But she wasn't there. She had walked away from him for a change. And he had no idea when, or if she had even heard what he said.

"Son of a bitch."

⚑

JANICE WAS HOPING to hide the fact that she was on Synergy from Nate as long as she could. She didn't need to hear him bitch about what a prima donna her racehorse was. She'd run out of there as soon as he agreed the retreat could come with them this morning. She hadn't wanted to push her luck and risk him changing his mind.

With nearly everyone in creation on this cattle drive, it looked more like spring roundup than just driving the cows from one field to another. They were short on horses. As it was, Pete was on Black Dahlia, who was looking to show off. It was a good thing Pete was an accomplished rider and could keep her focused.

Synergy wanted to run and beat the cattle to the pasture. Janice was the only one experienced enough to settle him into acting like a normal horse. She kept him wide and alongside the herd. That way, if he did act out, he was nowhere near the center of the pack. Luckily, he got his chance to chase a calf who decided to run the other way. Synergy was no barrel racer, but he got her there. And after three or four tries that she hoped her sisters and Nate didn't see, she managed to rope the runaway and guide him back to the meandering longhorns and Anguses. However, as they got close, Synergy got a little squirrelly. Luckily, Gayle was paying attention and she rode out to take the rope from her.

"Thanks," Janice said, trying to soothe Synergy. "I don't know what his problem is."

"There's something in the air," Gayle said.

Janice squinted up into the sky. She hoped not. The forecast said no rain, but the sky was darkening ominously. A little rain wouldn't kill them, but it wouldn't make for a pleasant day in the saddle. She had made sure the retreat had rain ponchos and bandannas. They'd make it through.

She hung back to see how Tracie and Regina were doing in the back. They looked sore and miserable, but still somehow determined to see this through.

"You did it," she said. "You won over Nate. You improved your riding skills and you're here."

Tracie gave her a thumbs-up, but Regina just held on to the reins.

"I can't wait for tonight," Regina said. "There's a peppermint schnapps with my name on it."

A spiked hot cocoa sounded good about now. Janice clamped a hand on her hat to keep it from sailing off as a gust of the wind that had just picked up blew through them.

Just then, an enraged squeal cut through the air. Janice looked up to see a mother sow pawing at the ground up ahead. The piglets started piping up as the boar crashed through the underbrush and rushed at the cattle.

"Oh no," Janice said.

Donovan rode hard, circling back behind the herd. It looked like he was trying to get a clear shot that wouldn't endanger the riders or the cows. Riding straight at the hogs, Donovan took aim and shot the boar. Ratcheting the lever on his rifle, he veered to take on the sow.

Synergy went wild, squealing almost as loud as the pig. The cows panicked and as Donovan's next shot took out the sow, everything happened at once. Synergy reared up, and if Janice hadn't been holding on tight with her thighs and on the reins, she would have tumbled off. When Synergy hit the ground, he tore off as if the gates had opened at Churchill Downs. She was powerless to do the one thing you should never do on a cattle drive. Ride through the center of the cows.

"Stampede!" Esteban called as Synergy bolted through them.

The panicked cows followed.

Janice could only hope everyone remembered what to do. And then thunder boomed to add to the cacophony of noise, and the rain came in a torrential downpour. She was terrified. Not just because Synergy was beyond reason. He'd only stop if he hit a rut and broke his leg or when he tired out. There was no catching him as he plowed ahead of the herd as if his life depended on it.

Hunched low over his neck and hanging on for dear life, she talked soothingly to him but it wasn't working. He remembered his dressage training and leapt over a fallen log instead of going around. Janice, however, wasn't used to doing that jump at such a high speed and she almost lost her seat. At this pace, it would feel like being ejected out of a crashed car if he threw her. She wanted to lead him toward the road the chuck wagon traveled, but with the rain and the wind and the mud—the mud was everywhere, in her nose, her mouth and eyes—she wasn't even sure where she was.

In the distance, she heard more gunshots or, with her luck, it could have been lightning strikes, as Synergy continued to wildly gallop away. Her hands were white-knuckled and Synergy was straining from running full out for this long. Janice was afraid he was going to collapse.

The rain was coming down in sheets and the damn fool horse finally slowed down to a canter and was frolicking in it.

"Come on, idiot," she said, trying to assert some control. But she was shaking too hard to make her authority stick. Pushing her wet hair off her face—she had lost her hat a ways back—Janice managed to circle Synergy back in the right direction at a fast canter. Her glasses were soaked and rain spotted, but at least she hadn't lost them. Synergy was winded, but not through panicking yet. Hopefully when they got back to the herd—what was left of it—they'd both be back under control.

A rider was coming toward them fast and Synergy danced sideways a bit when she tried to keep him on track. Through the wind and the rain, she recognized Nate. He was all right. Pissed, by the look of it, but all right.

"Sit up," he barked, and her spine straightened at his tone. She hadn't realized she had been slumped in exhaustion.

Twirling his rope, he came in close and looped it around Synergy's neck. Synergy fought him a bit, but Nate gave him plenty of slack.

"Don't give me any shit," he growled coming around

them.

She ducked and helped push the rope up and over her body so Nate was in control of the lead. "Are you talking to me or the horse?" she asked, ridiculously grateful to see him.

He muttered something under his breath that she was glad she couldn't hear.

Chapter Nineteen

"WELL, THAT WAS a clusterfuck to end all clusterfucks," Frank said, fists clenched and red-faced with anger.

Nate couldn't argue, but it could have been worse. No one was hurt. The cows were gathered up as soon as the rain stopped. It had made for a long day—a really long day. But they finished the roundup just after dark and after a lot of long, hot showers, still managed to have a secret-Santa party...with fresh grilled pork for dinner. It had been festive and in spite of himself, Nate had a pretty good time. It had been hard to watch Pete sticking so close to Janice, but she hadn't made an effort to seek Nate out alone so maybe she had come to her senses after all.

He hadn't expected to be so gutted about it.

The sisters made a pact not to tell their father about the stampede until after the party. And now it was time to face the music. Kelly and Trent had made themselves scarce with Alissa, because Alissa didn't like to hear PawPaw yell. Nate wished he was five years old again and could use that excuse.

Actually, that wasn't completely true. He wished he was five years old with parents like Trent and Kelly.

Nate slumped on the couch and hid a yawn. Even with Frank's temper and the finely tuned tension, Nate's eyes were closing and his head nodded a few times during the diatribe. Who would have thought that all he needed was Frank having a fit to send him off to dreamland? He would have pissed the old boy off a long time ago.

Frank caught him stifling a second yawn and it diverted his wrath from Janice to him. "I blame you. You told me that you had this under control."

"I'm good, but last time I checked, I don't control the weather or the migratory pattern of the feral hogs."

"That's another thing." Frank whirled on Donovan, catching him shoveling in a forkful of migas. "Why the hell are there so many feral pigs on my land?" Before Donovan could chew and swallow, Frank answered his own question. "It's because you run safaris so people can take pictures of them instead of shooting them." He yelled the last few words.

"Dad," Emily said, trying to soothe his temper. "Everything is fine."

"Everything is not fine. Everything is changing."

And that was the problem right there, Nate thought. Frank hated change, even if it was for the better.

"We're not any closer to being debt-free."

"That's not fair," Emily said. "We've paid off several outstanding bills."

"The wolves are still at our door," Frank said, flinging his hand. "Or hogs, in our case."

"Dad," Janice said, placing a hand on his arm. "I see that

you're upset. But like we told you, we're handling this."

"You're handling this by opening us up to an insurance nightmare. Any one of those women could have been trampled by a panicking steer."

"Fine. We won't do the cattle drive anymore. It wasn't the big dream come true that they all thought it would be, after all." Janice's attempt at humor fell flat.

"You're done with retreats. Tell your headshrinker friend and the ex-con that they're out. You can open up a dressage school, but I'm done with this touchy-feely crap."

Janice set her jaw. "No."

"Girl, you better not defy me on this."

They stood toe to toe, almost nose to nose, almost mirror images of each other. Nate looked at Sarah and she caught his eye. Tears shimmered in her eyes and Nate knew they weren't angry tears. Sarah hated conflict, so why she married Frank was beyond him. Nate knew from experience that she would wait out the battle and then pick up the pieces.

"Frank, you don't have a say in the matter," Nate said.

Sarah's eyes grew wide.

Janice whirled on him, gaping. "I don't need you to fight my battles."

Groaning, Nate stretched as he got up. "I know that, darlin'. I'm just tired of hearing Frank bitch about the same thing over and over again."

"You...you...traitor," Frank snarled. "First you go against my wishes and take advantage of my daughter."

"Whoa," Janice interrupted. "The advantage-taking was mutual."

Nate felt embarrassment color his cheeks, but it was only a matter of time before this was discussed. "We're consenting adults and you don't have a say in that matter, either."

Frank pounded his fist on the table, but no one jumped. That was how used to it they were. "I thought out of everyone here, you would support me on this."

"I'll admit, I thought you had the right of it. I even agreed with you."

"See," Frank said, gesturing at Janice.

"But then I saw how much the retreat helped those women. It's worth it to them. It's worth it to Janice. And it's bringing in the money to help with the bills. It's just not how you want to deal with the situation." Nate shrugged. "You signed off on it when you brought your daughters home and gave them the land. They've got legal documents to do what they want—and what they want is to help save your ranch from foreclosure."

"Our ranch," Emily said.

"All of our ranch," Sarah added.

"If they have their way—" Frank pointed at his daughters "—you and me will be out of a job."

"Frank, you're slowing down," Nate said as gently as he could.

Sarah winced. Even Donovan shook his head at him.

"You think? I can still kick your ass, boy. Let's go outside."

"I'm not fighting you. You're the closest thing I have to a father."

"Some father," Frank said bitterly. "I can't support my

family."

Nate snorted. "My own dad bet me in a poker game at Christmas and lost."

"Mine got my mother killed and used me as a shield and now is trying to get back into my life by renting Janice's retreat center," Donovan said.

The silence was so extreme you could hear a pin drop. He hadn't known that about Donovan, and this was the first time Nate had told anyone about his own Christmas story.

Janice was at his side and hugging him tight. Emily stood behind Donovan with her hands on his shoulders.

"So as far as fathers go, you're at least right up there with Billy King," Nate joked, referring to Trent's manager, who they'd just found out was also his father.

But Frank wasn't ready to stop fighting. He turned to Donovan. "Your father is Charlie Lincoln?"

Donovan nodded.

"The same man who is going to bring a bunch of his ex-cons on my land?"

Donovan caught himself mid-nod.

"And you all are okay with this?" Frank asked incredulously.

"I'm a long way from okay with it," Donovan said.

"See?" Frank gestured at Janice.

Nate slung his arm around her as she held on to him for dear life. He could feel her shaking and trying not to cry. He knew how angry that meant she was. He also knew that if Frank saw a glimpse of those tears, he would think he had won. Nate needed to end this conversation before Janice lost any credibility in her father's eyes.

"Unfortunately, it's not my decision to make," Donovan said. "I'll be here to help protect the family. And I'll be watching Charlie like a hawk. But Janice has done her due diligence and maybe, for once in his life, Charlie Lincoln is telling the truth."

Nate nodded. "And I think Rita Alvarez's therapy groups will get a lot out of Janice's program. They deserve to be here. And I'll be happy to take a trained group on a cattle drive again."

"You would?" Janice gaped up at him.

He nodded. "You did a great job. I was proud of them and of you, too."

She stood up on her tiptoes and kissed him.

"Right in front of me?" Frank said. "It's bad enough I had to hear it from the rest of Last Stand that you're sleeping with my daughter, but you're going to flaunt it in front of me? I thought we had an agreement."

"What agreement?" Janice narrowed her eyes at him.

"Your dad wanted me to encourage a relationship between you and Doc Pete."

"Dad," she said. "Since when are you giving Clara Perkins a run for her money?"

"Since, you're too blind to see a good thing that's right in front of you."

Janice shook her head. "I've seen it all along."

"So have I." Nate grinned down at her.

"This is ridiculous. Get out of my sight. All of you. And, Nate, consider if you really want to be working here anymore."

"Are you firing me?" Nate asked.

"No," Emily added. "He is not."

"I think you made your choice." Frank turned his back on them, and stormed into the living room.

Nate's gut clenched, but it wasn't as if he hadn't seen this coming. In a way, it was kind of a relief, now it was here. He knew that siding with Janice would set Frank off. And when Frank got set off, he exploded and sometimes people got wounded with the shrapnel.

"I guess that's that." He kissed Janice hard on the mouth and then turned on his heel and left the house.

He had worked damned hard for this ranch and it had been good to him. But he wasn't going to stay if Frank didn't want him here because he'd made the grave mistake of loving Frank's daughter. Nate was surprised that being cast out again didn't hurt as much as he remembered.

Instead of that hollow empty feeling, it was like his head had just stopped buzzing. After all these years, the shoe had dropped and Nate had survived it. But that could have been because Janice was in his heart and, now, he'd have to let her go. Because she couldn't leave her family until the ranch was safe from foreclosure.

Chapter Twenty

J ANICE TOUCHED HER lips, wondering what the hell that had meant.

"Don't just stand there," her mother said. "Go after him."

"I always have to chase after him. Why can't he chase after me for once?" Janice scowled.

"One more time. And then he can do the chasing. But if you don't go after him now," Sarah said, fussing with her apron, "I'm afraid he's going to leave for good this time."

Oh hell no. Not if she could help it. Running out of the house, she quickly caught up with him. "Where the hell do you think you're going?"

Nate stopped and looked up to the heavens, but if he thought divine intervention was going to stop her, he had another think coming. "You heard the man. I'm fired."

"Overruled."

"Last time I checked, it wasn't a democracy."

"He didn't actually fire you. And besides, he can't run this ranch without you and you know that."

"True." Nate nodded.

"But more important, he doesn't have the authority to

fire you. He gave over payroll and employment to Emily."

"I'm not going to stay somewhere I'm not wanted."

"You're wanted. I'm not letting him throw you off this ranch the way he did to Kelly."

"There's nothing you can do to stop that." He gave a half laugh. "Unless you decide to marry Pete. I'm sure if you marry Pete, all our sins will be forgiven."

"For the last damned time, I'm not marrying Pete for his money. If my father likes that idea so much, he can marry him. Besides, I think Rita would fight me for Pete, if it came down to it."

"My money is on you." He turned to go.

Janice clutched his arm and whipped him around. "Stop doing that. I swear I will rope and hog-tie you if you turn your back on me again."

His lips twitched. "Sounds kinky."

Whoa, that sent some serious images into her brain. But she refused to let him distract her. "If you leave, I'm coming with you."

"Darlin', if I leave, I'm leaving the state."

She folded her arms in front of her. "I'll go pack my bags." Then her arms dropped. "Unless, of course, you don't want me."

"Don't want you?" He wrapped his arms around her. "I've wanted nothing else for as long as I could remember. But I'm not going to take you away from your family. You gave up your life in Kentucky to help save this ranch. I'm not selfish enough to ask you to leave before that's settled."

Holding him tight, afraid he would disappear if she let

go, she said, "I don't care."

He gently put her at arm's length. "You have your business. It was a success. You'll be fully booked in no time and, soon, the ranch's ledger will be in the black. It will buy time for the wind farm to come into its own. You've done it. You and your sisters have done it. You just need to see it through. And deal with that grumpy old man."

"We can't do this without you," she said. "Please stay. You're not fired. In fact, Emily and I talked about it last night. After everything you've put up with, you deserve something special."

Nate looked her up and down and she felt the heat in his gaze down to her toes. "Special, huh?"

She wanted more than his eyes on her. "Your Christmas bonus is two weeks' paid vacation."

"You can't afford that."

"And I'm taking you to Hawaii."

"You definitely can't afford that," he said.

"That's what credit cards are for." Janice lifted her chin up at him defiantly.

He chuckled. "If Frank doesn't want me here…"

"Frank is pissed off that I'm not a large-animal vet. He's enraged that I'm not marrying for money. He's livid that I'm defying him about going through with Charlie's and Rita's retreats. It's got nothing to do with you. You just jumped in and took the heat."

Nate shrugged. "He doesn't get to be ugly to you girls. Not when I'm in the room."

Janice would not let this man go. She'd chase him forever, if she had to. Because he was only leaving since he thought it was the right thing to do. She'd show him that the right thing to do was to stay here with her. "In short, my father is throwing a tantrum that Alissa would be embarrassed to throw. And I don't care. He asked for help and we came. When he was in his sickbed, you stepped up. You nearly worked yourself to exhaustion for our family. He doesn't get to discard you like a used napkin. You're family. You're my family. I love you, you big jerk."

And then she started crying.

Damn it all. She almost got through this without the waterworks.

"I'm not crying because I'm sad," she hitched out, haltingly.

"I know. You're an ass-kicker. You're crying so you don't beat the hell out of your father. Or is it me?"

"Jury's out."

Nate held her until her sobs quieted.

"I love you, too," he said, kissing the top of her head. "But you're better off with Pete."

"Financially, maybe. But not in the long run. In the long run, it's always been you and me."

Taking in a deep breath, Nate held her tightly. "You're making it hard for me to go. If I do stay, I can't take a two-week vacation. There's too much work to do."

"Did I mention that I'm not going to wear anything but a bikini the entire time? Maybe not even that."

Nate blinked. "Hawaii, huh?"

"We'll go right after New Year's. Emily will have your

job covered by Esteban and the other ranch hands. You need to start giving Esteban more responsibility or you're going to turn out just like my father."

"What if I am already too much like him?" Nate sighed.

"He's a good man. That's not a bad thing. And I'll be there to tell you to knock it off when you're trying to fight my battles for me."

"I know you will." Nate kissed her again. "Still, who's going to look after the dogs if we go on vacation?"

"My mother loves her granddogs and that includes Daisy. Are you trying to come up with excuses to leave? If you don't want me, if you don't want this, just tell me. Stop blowing hot and cold. There's no need to hide or sneak around anymore. My dad knows we're doing it."

Nate snorted. "I can't tell you how I wish I'd kept my big-ass mouth shut in front of Highwater and the rest of the town."

Shaking her head, she said, "I'm not. We needed this push. Trent and Donovan will pitch in around the ranch. You need this vacation. And I need you."

She kissed him with all the desperation in her heart. After a moment, he kissed her back and her toes curled as she knew she had won.

"I love you, Janice Sullivan," Nate said between kisses. "I've loved you forever. But—" He held her face between his hands. "Could you forgive yourself if by marrying Pete you could have saved the ranch?"

"I don't care about the ranch as much as I care about you. If we lose the ranch, it will be sad. But if I lost you?"

She took in a shaky breath. "I don't ever want to think about that. You're my home. And whether it is here in Last Stand or on the next cattle ranch that needs a foreman, so be it."

"Do you think they need cowboys in Hawaii?" he asked.

"Let's find out," she said.

"Let's find out." He picked her up and carried her back to his cottage.

Kicking the door shut behind them, he eased her feet down to the floor. She molded herself against his strong body and kissed him. His mouth was feverish against hers. As he backed her into the bedroom, he peeled off her clothes. Janice sank down on the bed and watched him undress with greedy eyes.

"No more bullshit," she ordered. "This is it. I know what's good for me, and you're it."

"I'm going to hold you to that," he said, kicking off his boots and sliding his Levi's down his muscled thighs.

"Hold me to that, all right." She pulled him down next to her and ran her hands lovingly over the wild stallion tattoos on his arms.

He brushed a hot kiss down her cheek, to her neck. Janice wrapped her fingers around his cock and tugged on it playfully.

"Keep doing that and this'll be over before it starts."

"I've got time."

"We've got time," he said, smiling at her before focusing his attention on her chest.

Her nipples puckered for him even before he brushed the first kiss across them. His tongue teased them until the world became centered on the velvet feel of his hardness against her palm and the aching need inside her. When she thought she would beg, he kissed down to her belly and his cock slipped out of her hand. Missing the heavy weight of him, she stroked her fingers through his hair. He parted her legs and nipped at her inner thigh.

She giggled and opened her legs wide for more.

When he tasted her, he growled low in his throat. She arched into his mouth, loving the feel of his tongue lapping at her intimately. Holding his head there, Janice did some growling of her own and with her moans loud in the silence of his bedroom, she let the pleasure crest over her.

As he kissed his way back up her body, she stretched so she could reach the condoms in his bedside table. Pulling out a string of them, she tossed them on the bed. Nate paused at her breasts, sucking and massaging them until she went wild. Rolling him over on his back, she took him deep in her throat and gave him a taste of his own medicine.

"Get the condom out," she ordered, in between long slides of her tongue over him.

"Fuck," he groaned and tore open the package.

Bobbing her head a few times, she tortured him with hard sucks soothed with a swirl of her tongue. When his breaths grew ragged, she eased up and let him slide out of her mouth with a loud pop.

"Give me that," she said, taking the condom from him and fitting it on his cock.

"Whatever you want, darlin'. Now and always."

Straddling his body, she eased him into her and sank

down on him. They both savored the moment. Bracing herself on his shoulders, she rode him like a runaway race-horse. Nate's fingers bit into her ass and she loved the sounds he was making.

Throwing back her head, she laughed with pure joy and excitement. Nate was all hers and he wanted her just as much as she wanted him. She held him tight as tremors shook her body so hard, she thought she would fly apart. Sagging against his chest, she was boneless when he rolled her over and took her hard and fast.

His back was slick and slippery from their exertions. She entwined her legs with his and held on while the friction of him pumping in and out of her grew to a fever pitch inside her.

"Again," he said in her ear and the rawness in his voice threatened to tremble her over the edge again.

She clung tight, the bed making obscene creaking noises as the pace Nate sent stormed pleasure through every inch of her being.

"Please," she begged, unable to stop herself from coming. Eyes screwed shut, she cried out as she felt him twitch and jerk.

"Janice," he panted, pressing his forehead to hers. "You're stuck with me."

He rolled off her, clamping her close to his side.

"I'm going to hold you to that," she said, trying to get her breath back.

"Hold whatever you like," he said sleepily and then al-most immediately fell asleep.

Epilogue

J AMESON HOUSE WAS decorated in silver and gold. Practically everyone in town had shown up to support the fundraising ball to benefit the Last Stand Rodeo grounds and, more importantly, to see who the recipient of the rodeoing scholarship was going to be. The ballroom was full of dancers dressed in tuxedos and ball gowns. Nate was wearing a bolo tie with the brand-new boots Janice had bought him from Kelly Boots in Whiskey River. She was wearing a slinky red sheath that she wouldn't have had the guts to wear in public if her sisters hadn't forced her to buy it. Holding Nate's hand, she pulled him away from the bar where he was headed and out to the dance floor.

Kelly and Trent were already waltzing around. Alissa was standing on the top of her pawpaw's shoes as he danced with her. Her other grandfather, Billy, was waiting his turn and nursing a beer. Emily and Donovan were at the buffet table, no doubt loading up on the vegetarian delicacies they asked The Mustard Seed to provide so Emily didn't have to exist on crudités all night. Rita and Pete were talking with a group of their friends from Jameson Hospital. Her mother was chatting with Clara Perkins and Janice was so glad Clara wouldn't be turning her matchmaking eyes on her any longer.

"I can't dance," Nate said.

"Then just hold me close and sway to the music," Janice said, splaying her hand on his crisp leather vest. She admired the diamond ring he had given her for Christmas. Next year was going to be a great year for weddings. Kelly was going first in June. Then, Emily in October. But Janice had a special date in mind for her wedding.

"Nate, I was thinking."

"That always bodes trouble for me."

She deliberately stepped on his toe. "Hear me out anyway."

"Always," he said, brushing a kiss across her forehead.

"I decided on our wedding date."

"It's good of you to tell me. I might have missed it."

"I want to get married on Christmas Eve."

Nate stumbled.

"Next year," she quickly added.

"Yeah, I think your mother would kill us if we tried to put a wedding together in four days. Why do you want to get married on Christmas Eve?"

"Because, I want to replace your bad memory with a good one. When you start to think about your dad and how awful he was, I want you to realize that's in your past and every Christmas going forward, it's going to be you and me. We'll be surrounded by family and dogs and we'll make love all night long. And then the next day is Christmas. What could be better than that?"

"I can't think of a damn thing," he said, stopping. "Look up."

There was a big sprig of mistletoe hanging above them.

He kissed her breathless and probably longer than what was publicly appropriate, but Janice had no complaints. It wasn't going to be a serene marriage, but the passion would make up for the bumps in the road.

"I will always love you," Nate said, and kissed her forehead. "Are you crying again?"

"Shut up, asshole."

The End

If you enjoyed this book, please leave a review at your favorite online retailer! Even if it's just a sentence or two it makes all the difference.

Thanks for reading *The Cowboy's Heart* by Jamie K. Schmidt!

Discover your next romance at TulePublishing.com.

TULE
PUBLISHING

If you enjoyed *The Cowboy's Heart,*
you'll love the other books in….

The Three Sisters Ranch series

If you enjoyed *The Cowboy's Heart*,
you'll love these other Last Stand Christmas books!

Christmas Flowers
by Sasha Summers

Under the Mistletoe
by Eve Gaddy

Texas Christmas Tycoon
by Katherine Garbera

About the Author

USA Today bestselling author, Jamie K. Schmidt, writes erotic contemporary love stories and paranormal romances. Her steamy, romantic comedy, Life's a Beach, reached #65 on USA Today, #2 on Barnes & Noble and #9 on Amazon and iBooks. Her Club Inferno series from Random House's Loveswept line has hit both the Amazon and Barnes & Noble top one hundred lists. The first book in the series, Heat, put her on the USA Today bestseller list for the first time, and is a #1 Amazon bestseller. Her book Stud is a 2018 Romance Writers of America Rita® Finalist in Erotica. Her dragon paranormal romance series has been called "fun and quirky" and "endearing." Partnered with New York Times bestselling author and former porn actress, Jenna Jameson, Jamie's hardcover debut, SPICE, continues Jenna's FATE trilogy.

Visit her website at jamiekschmidt.weebly.com

Thank you for reading

The Cowboy's Heart

If you enjoyed this book, you can find more from all our great authors at TulePublishing.com, or from your favorite online retailer.

TULE
PUBLISHING

Printed in Great Britain
by Amazon